CLUB MAFIA – THE SAVAGE
A DARK MAFIA ROMANCE

STELLA ANDREWS

Copyrighted Material
Copyright © Stella Andrews 2022
Stella Andrews has asserted her rights under the Copyright, Designs and Patents Act 1988 to be identified as the Author of this work.
This book is a work of fiction and except in the case of historical fact, any resemblance to actual persons, living or dead, is purely coincidental.
All rights reserved. No part of this book may be reproduced or transmitted in any form without written permission of the author, except by a reviewer who may quote brief passages for review purposes only.

18+ This book is for Adults only. If you are easily shocked and not a fan of sexual content then move away now.

18+

NEWSLETTER

Sign up to my newsletter and download a free book

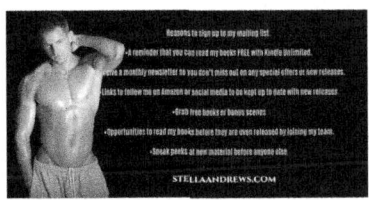

stellaandrews.com

THE SAVAGE

If you're not ready for the pain then don't seek the pleasure because Roses have thorns and thorns draw blood.

Ivan may be my name but I am best known as The Savage.
Born and bred Bratva heir and loving every delicious minute of my life.
That's why it was easy to kidnap the entitled Charlotte Richmond from her finishing school in England.
It was my pleasure to hide her away while her depraved father searched for her.

I have no heart, no emotion, and no morals.
She is a bargaining chip, a means to an end.
I will use her to set my friend's sister free from a madman.
An exchange if you like.

But this English Rose has deadly thorns and she's not going down without a fight.
Dark, dangerous, and full of depravity. This book will wrap you

in shadows until you can't bear the light. Scenes may upset some readers, you have been warned.

Bleeding romance and suspense, this book ticks all the boxes.
  High heat and scenes that are not for the fainthearted.

If you love a dark Mafia romance, you're in the right place.

CHAPTER 1

CHARLOTTE

ROSE HALL ACADEMY – ENGLAND

The trouble with study periods is they give your mind a chance to wander and today is no exception. As I sit twisting my pen in my hand and doing everything possible to avoid actually placing ink on the paper, my mind heads to the future and what's expected of me. What's expected of all of us currently doing time at Rose Hall Academy. A finishing school for the wealthy and a stop gap for students who don't have any purpose in life merely than to marry well and spend their inheritance.

Sighing, I stare out on the landscaped grounds of a very respectable place and long for a different future. Something cool, a little edgy perhaps. A million miles away from the one heading my way at lightning speed and there is nothing I can do about that.

"Psst, Charlotte."

I look up and twist my lips into a grin as I watch Rochelle rolling her eyes and nodding toward Mrs. Penrose, the study mistress, who appears to be sleeping. As she hides behind her huge tortoiseshell glasses, her head nods as the warm rays of the sun caress her skin and lull her into a state of unconsciousness.

Rochelle mouths, "Are you ok?"

I roll my eyes and nod as she throws me a despairing look of her own because we are both being 'finished off' as they say, so we can step into society and begin the hunt for a suitable husband that passes all the requirements laid down by our peers.

Like me, Rochelle would rather pull out her own teeth than entertain the cocky suitors that are lining up at the door, ready to make the best match they can. There is no love to be found in social climbing, just position and power, and we are the sitting ducks who allow it to happen or face the threat of being cut off and let loose in an unforgiving world.

Sighing, I stare out across the freshly mown lawn and watch the birds flying high in the sky and wish I was as free as them. They can go anywhere they want to with no restrictions and once again I allow the daydreams to make a bad day a whole lot better.

It starts as a gentle hum and then the sound gets louder, causing the class to look up and listen with eager ears.

This is different.

Mrs. Penrose jolts awake and glances up, appearing a little flustered as the noise grows ever closer.

Rochelle catches my eye and we both look out and see something hovering above the academy.

"What's happening?"

Martha Fraser asks the question we're all thinking, and Mrs. Penrose looks surprised. "I'm not sure. It sounds as if we have a visitor."

Helicopters aren't uncommon at Rose Hall. Many have

landed on the lawn while their occupant visits their daughter or head this way to enroll a new recruit to the damned.

The noise grows louder and, pushing decorum aside, the students push back from their desks and crowd against the window. Even Mrs. Penrose is curious, and the startled gasps move around the room like a Mexican wave as we witness a fleet of helicopters landing one by one on the huge lawn outside.

"My goodness." The clipped tones of Mrs. Penrose match our own shock and the chatter in the room increases as the students witness something new and, well, rather exciting.

We take our positions at every window and watch as the rotor blades ease and I hold my breath to see who steps out from the metal bird.

"It must be royalty." One eager voice whispers in awe and another one says, "Or from the government."

"Maybe it's a celebrity, a rock star or an actor." Another excited voice rings out and Rochelle nudges me as we stare in fascination as several men pour from the helicopters dressed entirely in matching black suits.

"Well, it's not the SAS. That's a crying shame."

Rochelle says under her breath, and I stifle a grin as Jemima Mortimer shrieks, "Wow, I wonder why they're here! It looks like an invasion."

Just the sight of the men in black shades, dressed head to toe in black, is giving me mafia vibes and it's only when my phone rings that it distracts me from the amazing sight outside.

Glancing down, I read a text from my mum and there is only one word.

Run

My heart starts beating, actually thumping so hard it almost hurts as I stare at the message and then look outside.

Another text comes through, and I turn and read it with an increasing sense of fear.

Meet me outside in the lane.
Don't let anyone see you leave.
You must move now; you don't have long.

My first thought is that my father's done something, and we need to run as a family. There is obviously no time for a family conference about this and I dread what could be tomorrow's headline.

My father is Lord Richmond and not a stranger to scandal and this must be another one of his mistakes hitting the headlines.

I look around and note that every eye in the room is glued to the unfolding drama outside, so without hesitating, I inch slowly toward the door into the corridor outside. My heart is racing, and I feel a rush of fear as I take the fire escape and make my way outside.

This must be serious; my mother wouldn't ask me to run if those men weren't here for me.

Just thinking of what that could mean spurs me on and as I push through the fire escape, I slam it loudly behind me. Luckily, the rest of the school is otherwise entertained, and I sprint the short distance to the tree-line, hoping like hell nobody can see me and raise the alarm.

The wall that surrounds Rose Hall Academy is designed to keep us in and intruders out, but we discovered a hole in it a while ago leading to the lane outside. Ivy has grown over the space that was the result of a car hitting it late one night a few years ago. The school never had it repaired, and I've lost count of the number of girls who have snuck out and met the local lads for a night of sin. Not me though. Not good little Charlotte Richmond, who plays by the rules. Maybe that's why I feel so afraid now. This isn't like me. This *isn't* me and as I squeeze through the thick ivy, I wish it was anyone else but me right now.

I scrape my elbow on a bramble and a nettle stings me at the same time and I curse my father for his recklessness. Why can't he just be happy with what he's got instead of the numerous affairs he appears to thrive on that always make it into the tabloids?

Feeling quite cross about the whole situation, I look down the lane for my mother's car and note a black Range Rover parked halfway down.

Quickly, I run toward it and hope she has a good explanation for this and as soon I reach it, the door flies open and before I know what's happening, I am pushed inside.

By the time I open my mouth to scream it's too late because the door closes, and I hear the locks engage and then a bag is placed over my head and tied securely at the neck before my wrists are bound and I am strapped into the seat as the car speeds away.

I have never been so frightened in my whole life and the fear only intensifies when a rough voice whispers in my ear, "You're mine now."

CHAPTER 2

IVAN

As plans go, this one was executed perfectly, and I'm quite smug as we speed away from Rose Hall Academy with the target neatly secured by my side.

In fact, the whole plan was a stroke of genius, even if I do say so myself.

It wasn't difficult to steal Lady Richmond's phone while she lunched at the Savoy. The distraction at the school was easy to arrange and I laugh to myself when I think of Yuri playing the part of a father searching for a school for his daughter. It wasn't difficult to persuade him either because he loves nothing more than making an entrance and when I told him why, he couldn't sign up quickly enough.

Lord Richmond has become a problem for the Bratva that is a difficult one to solve. It always is when it involves a high-profile customer who owes us, so this was the perfect excuse to kidnap his daughter and demand he pay up to get her back.

It's a shame he never will because there's a much higher bidder for the woman beside me, which will set Winter free and bring her home to us where she has always belonged.

As I sit back in my seat, I wonder what's running through

this girl's mind right now. She must be fucking terrified, and I feel bad for her. Then again, she has lived a life of privilege to this point and so any guilt I have is quickly pushed aside because it will do her good to see how hard life can be for most of the population. Me included. My friends included and a little discomfort for once in her life is just the consequences of a very bad action.

I'm surprised that she doesn't scream, struggle even, but it's as if she's frozen in place. Maybe she's fainted, stopped breathing perhaps, but as I run my eye across her chest, I see it heaving as she struggles to remain in control.

I'm not happy about this, but there are always casualties in every war, and she is just one of them. A bargaining chip in a deadly game and unfortunately for her, the man she is heading toward is a bastard at it.

The car screeches into the private airfield where our jet is standing by and as we stop in front of the steps, I waste no time in flinging the door open and heading around to her side.

As I pull her roughly out, I toss her over my shoulder and growl, "Move one inch and I'll knock you out."

Once again, she stiffens and I'm a little disappointed about that. She's making it too easy. Where is the fight I love? This is almost boring, and I consider slapping her ass just to get a reaction, but instead I haul her up the steps over my shoulder and content myself with dropping her into her seat and securing her bound wrist to it with handcuffs.

The door closes behind us and the engines start and just five minutes after we arrived at High Baron airfield, we are speeding down the runway with a very precious cargo onboard.

Once the plane is in the air, I relax and, being slightly curious, I untie the fastening around her neck and pull the bag off in one swift move.

I'm not sure who is more shocked and, as I stare into the

most bewitching eyes I have ever seen in my life, I lose the power of speech.

Deep blue eyes stare at me with horror, the tears glistening in them like pools of crystal water. Like a startled fawn, this woman looks at me with fear and her lower lip trembles as she regards me with an expression that makes me feel like the biggest bastard in the world.

Her long blonde hair is tied back in a ponytail and several strands have escaped their binding and trail across a face that is as white as snow. She looks utterly terrified and as those long lashes bat in my direction, I try so hard to remain focused.

"Charlotte Richmond." Perhaps I should have checked we had the right girl before we left and relax when she nods.

With a deep sigh of relief, I say roughly, "Just do as I say at all times, and this will be over quickly."

She looks to the floor, and I wonder what she's thinking and leaning forward, I grasp her face in my hand and lift it to stare into my eyes. She flinches at the contact and it's like holding a frightened animal in my hand and I feel like the biggest bastard as I say roughly, "You are my prisoner and must do everything I say otherwise you'll regret it. Do I make myself clear?"

She nods and as I hold her face in my hand, I stare at a beauty I wasn't expecting. In fact, I don't think I've ever met a woman quite like Charlotte Richmond before. The girls I'm used to have more sass than sense and would probably be screaming and complaining by now. Not her, though. She just regards me with a startled look in her eye that makes it even worse and so I drop my hand and say abruptly, "Get some sleep. This will be a long flight."

While I lean back in my seat, I wait for her reaction, and she seems almost shy as she whispers, "Where are we going?"

"Russia."

Her eyes widen and the shock in them makes me smile as I shrug. "It's the perfect place to lose a life."

"My life?" She appears more intrigued than afraid, and I nod.

"I need to keep you out of the spotlight. Somewhere nobody would think to look for you, and I know the perfect place."

"But why?"

She's curious and I owe her that at least, so I sigh and lean back in my seat.

"Your father owes us money and his credit limit has expired. He missed his last few payments, and we need to persuade him to pay up."

"My father owes you money."

She appears shocked about that, causing me to lean forward and stare into her bewitching eyes and snarl, "What's the matter princess? Are you worried your inheritance is under threat?"

For the first time, I see a little fire in her expression as she says angrily, "I couldn't give a fuck about my inheritance."

I love getting at least one reaction from her and can't help saying, "Your type is all the same."

I sneer and curl my lip and the flush to her cheeks has more to do with anger than anything as she hisses, "You know nothing about me. How dare you judge before knowing the facts, which as it happens, you never will, so do what you must, get your blood money and do it fast because the sooner I'm away from such a judgemental arsehole the better."

"You mean asshole." I smirk and love watching her eyes blaze with fury as she snaps, "Arsehole. I'm English, remember."

She pointedly turns away and I watch her silently fuming in her seat as she sits straight backed and defiant, not even trying to free her wrists.

Shrugging, I stand, needing to take a piss and, without any more words, leave her to stew and head to the rear of the aircraft.

CHAPTER 3

CHARLOTTE

*H*ow has this happened? One minute I'm daydreaming my day away and the next I'm in the middle of a Netflix movie. I should be frightened, tearful and pleading for my life, but I'm shocked to discover I'm merely intrigued. Things like this don't happen to girls like me. Men like him don't happen to girls like me and when the hood was ripped from my head, my first reaction was stunned surprise.

Throughout the car journey, I imagined a very different captor. His voice alone alerted me to a strange accent. American laced with one I couldn't place. I never imagined he would be so young. He can't be far from my own age and, quite frankly, he took my breath away.

Close cropped hair and rough stubble grazing his chin. Dressed in combats and a khaki t-shirt that made him look more like a soldier than anything else. The intricate ink on his forearms appeared to trail underneath his t-shirt and the muscles that it clings to made me experience something I never have before. Interest.

The person facing me wasn't a boy, he was all man who

intrigued me more than anything and made me forget to be afraid. For some reason, I was caught up in the drama and even being tied and handcuffed to a chair doesn't scare me as much as it should. Perhaps I'm delusional and don't understand how serious this situation is.

Remove me from life he said, well, I couldn't have asked for more if I had my own wish. I want removing from my life. It bores me to tears anyway and my heart hasn't stopped thumping since the moment I got the text.

The trouble is this guy rubs me up the wrong way. He's so dismissive, curt, and crude and I can tell he doesn't think much of me from that heiress comment. The fact he's right has nothing to do with it and I wonder about him. Looking back on the helicopters and the men in black suits, it tells me I was right when the word mafia entered my head. He is one of them. It's obvious and yet I'm still not scared. I've been kidnapped for ransom and now I know they need me alive for that I can rest a little easier. I must be having a dark dream because why am I not scared shitless? What's happening to me?

The shiver of excitement that's building is telling me I'm not all mentally there. Things like this shouldn't excite me. I should be cowering in fright and begging for my life, but I'm more intrigued than anything. Then there's him. The brutal Russian/ American, who knows what, is attracting me way more than I care to admit.

My heart jumps when he returns holding a bottle of whiskey that he is draining at the source causing me to sneer, "Don't you have glasses in Russia?"

I can't stop baiting him and he shrugs before dropping into the seat opposite and taking a swig, maintaining eye contact with me the whole time.

Setting it down, he smirks. "Want some."

He laughs out loud, probably due to the horror that must

show on my face, and as he leans closer, the stench of whiskey hits me, causing me to recoil slightly.

"What's the matter princess? Whiskey too hard for you. I've got Champagne if you prefer, Prosecco maybe, or perhaps some coke, in a line or a glass. Both can be arranged."

I shrug and say primly, "Water will be fine."

"What if I don't have water?"

"Then you'd be lying."

I won't back down and play the victim, and he stares at me long and hard for a moment and then nods. "Water it is."

As I experience a strange sense of victory, I congratulate myself on this small win and feel quite smug as he heads off and returns with a bottle of water.

"What, no glass?" I tilt my head with a challenge in my eye and then, to my horror, he reaches down and grabs my ponytail, and tilting my head back with his face inches from mine, he says gruffly, "Open your mouth."

"But…"

"I said open your mouth, princess."

He thrusts the plastic bottle between my lips and tilts it, so the water pours down my throat, causing me to choke a little. As I cough, the water drips from my mouth and as his hold tightens, it causes the tears to spill from my eyes.

"You're hurting me." I gasp and he says roughly, "I know."

Once again, he tips the liquid, and it fills my mouth, causing me to gulp quickly before I choke even more.

Then, without warning, he pulls the bottle away and, with his lips close to mine, whispers, "I control you, Princess. You cut the smart-ass remarks, do as I say and don't believe your opinion counts. There are no free rides when I'm around and if you think you have the right to talk down to me, your stay will be an extremely unpleasant one. So can the attitude, shut the fuck up and talk to me with respect because the minute you do none of those things, I will spank your ass so hard you won't stop experiencing the burn for weeks. Do I make myself clear?"

I nod and he tightens his hold on my ponytail and pulls my head back, growling, "I can't hear you."

"Yes, perfectly clear."

He drops me like a hot poker and pushes me back roughly in my seat and then storms off down the plane to what I can only imagine is another cabin behind us, leaving me reeling.

That was so intense. I really thought he was going to hurt me, and he did, in a way. My pride has certainly taken a battering and it may take some time to get my breath back, but the point hit home. I'm a prisoner and regardless of my stupid, immature behavior, I am in a very dangerous situation indeed and should remember that.

Thankfully, he leaves me alone, and it gives me time to reassess my situation. I wonder if my parents have discovered I'm missing. The fact he texted me from my mother's phone is still disturbing me. Did they tie her up somewhere, and she's still missing too? Is she ok and what about my father? Does he know about this and if he does, what will he do?

I'm guessing he'll raise the money, not that I'm deluded enough to think it's about me. No, Lord Richmond lives a life of smoke and mirrors and hides behind them most of the time. The dashing, entitled lord in public and obviously a debauched lecherous lothario in private.

I wonder if my mother knows about his double life. I'm not even sure she does because they always put on a united front of appearing so happy. Surely this guy has it wrong. They must be thinking of another man entirely and got their names mixed up.

My head hurts so much with trying to figure it out and as the lights in the cabin dim and the day turns to darkness, somehow, I fall into a troubled sleep.

CHAPTER 4

IVAN

I had to walk away for my own sanity and her protection. There was something that riled me about the supercilious way she looked at me. As if I was nothing, an undesirable and the dirt beneath her Jimmy Choo's. Not that she's wearing those, of course. After all, she's wearing a fucking uniform, for Christ's sake. That alone should put me off, but she's still the most intriguing woman I have ever met, and I've met a few. Charlotte Richmond fascinates me because she has a bravery I wasn't expecting.

Most women look at me with either fear or lust. Not interest as if I'm a pet project she needs to figure out. I thought the whiskey would help, but it just lowered my guard and released the savage that lives inside me most of the time.

"Problem boss?"

Leo interrupts my dark thoughts, and I shake my head.

"Nothing I can't handle."

"So, what's the plan when we land?"

I sense the interest around me because my men are as intrigued by this situation as I am.

All they've been told is we are kidnapping the lord's

daughter for ransom and need to hide her until he pays up. They don't know the real reason I targeted Charlotte Richmond, and I wonder how they would react if they discovered what it was.

"You leave us at Norilsk, and I'll call when we need a ride."

The fact he looks relieved about that makes me smile to myself. Dubbed the most depressing place to live on earth, Norilsk can only be reached by air as there are no roads in. My family keeps an apartment there if we need to lie low and I wonder what Miss. Richmond will make of the rather basic standard of living we enjoy there. Unlike our many other homes around the world, this one is pure minimalism. The bare essentials only because it's not a place we frequent much. Hell, I've only been here once myself and that was as a punishment for answering my father back. No, this will not be an enjoyable stay at all and that gives me way too much pleasure just imagining my perfect princess slumming it for once in her life.

After playing poker with Leo and a couple of my men, I yawn loudly and nod toward the cabin at the rear of the aircraft.

"I'm grabbing some sleep while I can. Make sure our guest remains uncomfortable and if anything happens to her, I will not be happy, understand?"

The spark of fear in Leo's eyes reminds me how much they fear me. Ivan Volkov, the son of Konstantin Volkov, Bratva Pakhan, the head of the largest crime syndicate in Russia and I'm his unlucky heir. He started life in the KGB and soon progressed to organized crime with the full support of the government. An oligarch of the deadliest kind and a man many call the biggest bastard in Russia.

It amuses me how easily he agreed to help and set about contacting one of his spies in London to help stage the kidnap.

Pavel Semenov was only too happy to oblige because he has

always sought approval from the motherland and would have pissed gold if my father asked him to.

The fact I can't stand any of them is a minor irritation, which is why I was so keen to join Club Mafia, along with my friends from college who are my brothers from other mothers. We have our own plan, and it involves world domination.

Angelo, the boss, has already sorted his shit out and is now the don in charge of the Sontauro family in Boston. Flynn Vasquez is the second one of us who has stepped up and is the reason the hapless Miss. Richmond is my guest. I wonder what she would do if she discovered the real reason she's here. Not a lot, I'm guessing, and it amuses me to choose my moment to wipe that smug grin from her face when she learns what her future holds. Hell on earth is a place, and it's preparing her room.

I leave my men to drink vodka and gamble and head to the cabin reserved for members of the Volkov family only.

Inside is a huge double bed that will do nicely because I have been up for sixteen hours already and need sleep and a shower, so I'm ready to entertain the angel I'm about to sacrifice.

I'M NOT sure how long I slept, but as I wake the sun is rising and floods the cabin with its warm rays. As I stretch out, I allow my mind to adjust and remember a successful mission yesterday. Noting how hungry I am, I swing my legs to the floor and walk naked into the shower room attached to the cabin. My father likes his luxury, which I am glad about because the hot jets of water are extremely welcome as they wash away the sleep and dust from the day before.

My bag is on hand to retrieve a fresh set of clothes and as I run my fingers through the jagged edges of my hair, I reach for the toothbrush.

As I stare at myself in the mirror, I raise a small smile because now I've slept, I'm a lot happier about this mission. The fact the girl is so stunning certainly helps, and I'm keen to drag that bad-assed attitude out to play to keep me amused. Maybe she will prove a worthy adversary, I certainly hope so because life could get boring very quickly if she isn't.

I head outside and the flight attendant is hovering by the door, looking as if she wants to jump me. I don't miss the desire lit in her eyes, or the small smile of encouragement she flashes me as she whispers huskily, "Is there anything you need, sir?"

"Food and lots of it. Coffee too. I'll take it with the girl."

If she is disappointed, she covers it well and just nods. "Of course, sir."

I walk past my men who are stretched out on their reclining seats trying to sleep and as I approach the front of the aircraft, I feel like a bastard when I see Charlotte sleeping upright with her head to one side. Her wrists are still handcuffed to the seat, and I can see angry red marks surrounding them as the metal grazes her skin.

I'm not even sure why I kept her chained up like an animal and for some reason it doesn't sit well with me, so I grab the key from my pocket and carefully insert it into the lock, taking care not to disturb her.

As I work, I can't help but stare at a woman who surprises me every time I look at her. Her long lashes brush against her pale skin and her lids flutter as she somehow manages to dream. Her soft sigh does something to me inside and I blame the fact I haven't been laid in a week. I briefly wonder whether to take the stewardess up on her obvious invitation, but she doesn't even compare to this beauty in front of me.

Then I'm surprised and taken off guard when a sharp blow

lands flush against my cheek, causing my head to snap sideways and the pain makes me wonder if I've broken a bone.

Recovering quickly, I stare into two pools of fiery rage as the English rose, who looked so perfect a moment ago, stares at me with all the fury of Hades in her eyes.

"You fucking bastard."

She says it so low I almost think I've heard wrong and then she hisses, "You are treating me like a dog. Do you really believe I have a fucking parachute hidden inside this school uniform? Do you envision I'm packing a machine gun to kill you all stone dead before I take over the controls of this aircraft and fly myself back to Rose Hall frigging academy for young ladies?"

For some reason, it makes me smile which only serves to increase her anger as she takes another swipe and as I catch her wrist, she gasps when I jerk her body to mine and pull her hands behind her back.

I whisper angrily, "You just earned that spanking."

"You wouldn't."

The fact her voice has risen an octave and I feel her tremble against me, causes a chain reaction I never saw coming and in one swift move, I pull her across my knee and pulling up her skirt, deliver five resounding blows to her ass in rapid succession.

Her gasp of pain doesn't deter me and when her ass is red enough to remind her how serious this is, I pull down her skirt and growl, "Now play nice and I'll be the perfect gentleman. Take another shot at me and it will be worse next time. Do you understand?"

"Yes." The word is edged out through gritted teeth and as the stewardess heads our way with a tray of sweet-smelling waffles, I keep one arm on Charlotte and nod to the stewardess to set the tray down on the table at the side.

She looks at Charlotte with curiosity while pouring two

coffees before leaving with a soft, "Call me if you need anything else."

The fact she fucks most of my men is enough to strike her off my list and I nod with a dismissive, "Thanks. I will."

As she heads through the curtain, Charlotte tries to pull away from me and I growl, "Not fucking likely. You act like a child; I'll treat you like one. Now open your mouth."

"Why?" She sounds fearful as I spear a piece of waffle onto the fork and hold it against her lips. "So you can eat, of course. You must be starving."

Against her better judgment, she can't resist temptation and as she takes the food from the fork, she stares into my eyes the entire time with a bravery that impresses me all over again.

I stare at her ruby red lips as she chews the food, and the light dancing in her eyes tells me she's relishing every minute of it.

I'm enjoying this way too much for comfort and with a heavy sigh, I push her from my lap, so she falls to a heap on the ground.

"What was that for?"

She winces as she experiences the mark of my hand on her ass, and I grin.

"What's the matter, angel, missing me already?"

She glowers, which only makes me laugh and I shrug. "I thought you'd be happy. What's the matter? Are you getting attached?"

"In your dreams, asshole." She mimics my accent and as I frown, she scoots away quickly and makes to stand, unknowingly flashing me the perfect view of her rather large panties.

It makes me laugh again and she snarls, "What's so funny?"

"Your underwear."

Her face flames as red as her ass, which only makes me laugh more, and she glares at me furiously.

"You have no business looking at or touching my underwear. Anyway, the uniform is also extended to our knickers, if you must know. I had no choice."

"Knickers?" I shake my head and she huffs. "What do you call them then?"

"Panties."

She shrugs. "Call them what you like. Mine are of no concern to you."

She sits in the seat as far away from me as possible, yet I don't miss the yearning in her eyes when she stares at the breakfast tray. Grabbing a pastry, I savor the mouthful I tear with my teeth, and she mutters, "Savage."

This alone makes me laugh out loud and says shortly, "What's so funny?"

"The fact you called me by name."

"Savage? Your parents must have really hated you."

"Many do princess, and I'm guessing I've just added you to that list."

"You got that right."

She turns away and looks out of the window and despite myself, I heap as much food on a plate as it will hold and pour her a mug of coffee.

"Here, eat your breakfast in peace. I have business to discuss with my men."

Her head jerks back, and she fails to hide the gratitude in her eyes as she receives the plate and whispers, "Thank you." before looking down.

Once again, it makes me smile because even under extreme circumstances, my pretty little princess still maintains her manners.

As I leave her to eat, it's with a rare smile on my face because there is something about Charlotte Richmond that makes me happy. Possibly because she is easy to antagonize, and I love seeing the anger flare in her pretty eyes and briefly wonder what it would be like to fuck a girl like her. I say girl, but underneath that prissy uniform is a woman and I'm guessing one that has yet to discover how powerful she can be. It's just a shame her destiny lies in another direction and just picturing the bastard we are sending her to is enough for me to keep my distance, no matter how delectable a treat she would be.

CHAPTER 5

CHARLOTTE

I have never been so hungry. Two years of school meals at Rose Hall makes this a feast fit for a queen. Not that I would tell the savage that. His ego needs no further stroking, and yet there is something wickedly enjoyable about our banter. He appears to like it too and I wonder if I'm falling head-first into madness because why would I enjoy conversing with a rough villain like him?

As I chew the mouth-watering croissant, I glance out of the window and see nothing but clouds beneath us. It's as if I am on top of the world and not lower down in hell. My mind drifts to our destination and I experience a tingle of alarm because Russia is definitely not a place I have ever had on my bucket list. It's always been so mysterious, so dangerous even, and now I'm heading that way with some of its most dangerous men.

I'm hoping that customs will demand my passport and it will alert the authorities to my illegal status. I certainly hope so and picture myself heading home on a British Airways jet, enjoying afternoon tea in no time. Not this private jet that was probably bought with blood money. Drugs, probably, and crimes I don't even want to think of.

The stewardess heads back into the cabin and I don't miss her curious stare and smile weakly, hoping to alert her to my predicament. Maybe she can get the captain to radio ahead and have the local police meet the aircraft.

"Hi."

I hand her my plate and she looks away. It takes me by surprise, and I clear my throat.

"I'm sorry, it's well, I…"

She leans down and hisses, "Don't talk to me—ever. Do you want to get us both killed?"

My eyes widen at the animosity in her voice, and she glares at me angrily before clearing away the breakfast things and storming from the cabin.

How rude. I am incensed because manners cost nothing and yet what has made her so afraid? They will kill us. For talking. What sort of fucked up shit show have I fallen into?

Now I'm unsettled and bracing myself for my imminent murder, which makes me nauseous. Remembering my back chat leaves me cold because what was I thinking antagonizing my captor? I really should face the reality of my situation and keep my sarcastic mouth shut to preserve my life.

About thirty minutes later, my ears start popping, telling me we are beginning our descent and now I'm nervous for a different reason. We're here. Wherever that may be and where I'm going may not be so welcoming.

I jump when the savage, or whatever his real name is, heads back into the cabin and takes his seat, shouting, "Make sure you're strapped in, we're about to land. It may be a little bumpy."

I do as he says, hoping he hasn't remembered I'm not tied up and I briefly wonder if I can somehow use that to my advantage. I haven't missed the gun tucked in the back of his combats or the hunting knife he likes to spin in his hands. If the landing is bumpy, I may get a chance to seize his weapons and turn them on him instead. I already know how badly that would pan out, for me, anyway and so with a sigh, I grip the seat arm rests and prepare myself for my darkest hour.

* * *

HE WASN'T KIDDING and as the plane thumps onto the tarmac and the pilot applies the brakes, it's as if every bone in my body has been jarred. My heart is beating so fast it may just kill me and as we screech to a stop, I swear I see smoke outside.

A low laugh turns my attention to my captor, who appears to have enjoyed that and catching me looking, he grins. "Always an experience." Then he winks and for some reason, it floors me a little. Regardless of who he is, he is still probably the most attractive man I have ever met in my life and part of me is happy to let him star in my fantasizes for one brief delicious moment but then again, he's a savage, he told me that himself and my arse is reminding me just what a savage does for fun around here.

I don't think I will ever forgive him for that act of humiliation and pasting a scowl on my face, I stare out at a place that wouldn't win any prizes in the top ten destinations to visit in the world.

It's bleak but doesn't appear that cold. I'm not sure why but I was expecting it to be icy, snowy even. I think I've always pictured Russia that way, but this looks like England on a gray dull day, and it's almost like home.

The plane taxis to a stop and as the door opens, a sudden gust of wind enters the cabin and makes me shiver. The savage looks at me and frowns and calls out something in Russian which sounds quite sexy on him, and I'm surprised when another man enters the cabin dressed in a black suit like the ones at Rose Hall and thrusts a coat at him.

"Here, princess, you may need this."

He pulls me to my feet and helps me into the oversized black woolen coat and fastens it securely. To my surprise, he looks at me with concern before lifting his hand and tucking my hair behind my ear. Just this one simple act of care does something to me inside. It breaks down my defenses in a far more brutal way than any act of violence. It makes the tears well in my eyes and the power of speech to leave me because in a matter of seconds, I have reverted to being that young girl who is alone and scared of the dark. The fact he looks concerned almost undoes the stitching of the armor I've constructed and when he leans in and whispers, "Don't worry, I'll take care of you."

It makes me grip his hand a little tighter.

CHAPTER 6

IVAN

Now we are here in Mother Russia, it breaks me all over again. I hate coming home. It's never a pleasure and bringing a woman like Charlotte here seems wrong on every level. Girls like her don't deserve the harshness of my homeland. She deserves sunshine and luxury. It's all she's used to, and I appear to have conveniently forgotten my animosity toward her.

I now want to protect her, which makes me an idiot because the only one she needs protecting from here is me.

The usual black car awaits us and as we walk down the steps, my ever-present guards are standing by, looking out for danger. It's how we live. I've never known any different unless you count the glorious time I spent at Rockwell Academy. There I was free to be a college kid like everyone else. I had friends, like me, who are jaded with this life. We formed a close bond and when Winter came to stay with her friend Emma, every single one of us learned the importance of family. The fact Winter was stolen before graduation and forced to marry a man old enough to be her father tore us apart. We made a vow to set her free and Charlotte Richmond is the key to that because the man who holds the woman we love with all our hearts, is Charlotte Richmond's biological father, Massimo Delauren.

Possibly the most feared Mafia Don in the world and definitely the maddest. His reputation alone causes grown men to shake in fear. A sadist, a cold-blooded killer who makes it his hobby. A psychopath and a man with zero morals. That is Charlotte's future, and for the first time since learning of this plan, I'm not liking my part in this. In fact, just imagining sending this innocent angel into hell is making me doubt I can see this one through.

I can tell she's frightened. Her silence tells me that and the way she is gripping my hand so hard tells me she's sticking with the devil she knows.

As we step into the car, she shrinks into the corner as if she hopes to remain invisible and I sigh inside. Now I feel like a bastard and that wasn't supposed to happen.

The driver pulls away from the aircraft, leaving my men to continue their journey back to a much more hospitable location, and I briefly wonder if I've thought this through. Norilsk is the perfect place to hide among the menagerie of apartment buildings in a town accessible only by air. However, Massimo Delauren has a far-reaching grip and possibly even has spies in Russia who would tell him this is the most likely bolt hole for any kidnapper hoping to stay under the radar.

We are silent as we speed through the streets, and I'm guessing Charlotte must be wondering how we bypassed customs. The fact my father is so powerful means most government officials are in his pocket and we come and go freely and could bring a container of heroin into the country and nothing would be said.

We take the short drive through the city and Charlotte says nothing at all. She just stares out of the window, and I wish I could be proud of my country, but this is a world away from her usual surroundings.

The silence that sits between us is awkward and threatening and I doubt that will change anytime soon. Now Charlotte will face the reality of her situation and I'm the idiot who was available for the job.

* * *

WE REACH the apartment set in the heart of the city and I look around with a sinking feeling. I hate this place. I could have taken her anywhere. We own enough luxurious homes that are well guarded all around the world that would have been perfect. Even the super yachts dotted around the globe are better options. It would have been better if we had sailed into the middle of the ocean and been perfectly protected, but I chose Sodom and Gomora and I'm the idiot who must deal with that.

As I help Charlotte from the car, she says in disbelief, "We're staying here."

I follow her glance and take in the huge apartment blocks crowding the city, each one a carbon copy of the next one. Old, decaying and built from concrete, these blocks are enough to make the happiest, most positive person in the world depressed. All around us are litter and discarded objects. A burned-out car mixing with debris from an overflowing dumpster act like the filthiest work of art. Corrugated iron on gray stone facades, speak of more decaying inside. Even the concrete walls are crumbling, and the iron fencing looks rusty in parts and bent out of shape.

The block we are staying in looks as if it barely survived a bomb attack, and I sigh heavily and guide her toward the door leading into hell.

"I don't think…" She falters and stops dead in her tracks

and just the pitiful edge to her voice strikes me deep where I never knew I had a heart.

"It's fine, you'll get used to it and hopefully it won't be for long."

Gripping her hand hard, I pull her with me and as we enter the dark, gloomy building, it's as if the prison gates are slamming shut behind us.

We head inside and rather than risk the ancient elevator, we take the concrete steps to the top floor. Cursing my father for keeping this place and not renovating it into luxury, I prepare myself for an ordeal of the most uncomfortable kind.

By the time we reach the top floor, even I'm out of breath and Charlotte looks as if she's about to pass out and I growl irritably, "Hurry up, the sooner we get inside, the better."

"You think?"

Her smart reply doesn't help my mood and as I unlock the many locks on the door, I take a deep breath and prepare for a hellish few days.

Inside smells dusty and I'm guessing nobody has been here for several months and I don't blame them. The fading wallpaper has definitely seen better days and the mismatched carpet looks as if it's bald in places.

Sighing, I look around at the old-fashioned light fittings that I'm not convinced would pass any safety check and the ornate mirrors with years of dust trapped in their gilded edges.

Charlotte gasps and says in a small voice, "Is this it?"

"Of course this is it." I snarl. "What did you expect, Buckingham Palace?"

I'm irritable and antsy and start prowling around the apartment, wishing I could smash it to pieces.

To my surprise, her soft voice wafts across the room like a summer breeze on a stifling day. "Then we must make the best of it. Show me to the kitchen. There must be some cleaning things here. Perhaps I can smarten it up a little and brighten the place up. It may not be so bad."

Her voice shakes as she forces a brightness to it and I snarl, "Then you're deluded if you believe anything can smarten this shithole up, but be my guest and try."

I head to the crumbling cupboard in the corner where I retrieve a bottle of vodka and, tearing the cap off, I chug down a strong measure.

"That won't help the situation." She sounds disapproving and I growl, "Maybe not, but it may make it bearable. Want some."

I thrust the bottle toward her, and she sniffs. "I'd prefer a cup of tea. Do you think we should find a shop to get some milk? Unless there is a well-stocked fridge, that is."

"You're going nowhere."

She looks a little shocked as I storm pass her into the small kitchen and wrenching open the door see it's crammed full as requested. We employ someone local who looks after this place and stocks up on demand and there is enough food in here to last for several weeks. The cupboard is no exception and as I open it, I see it is stocked with everything I requested.

Charlotte gasps over my shoulder. "Is that English tea, or is it a mirage?"

I conceal the grin her words create and pull the box down.

"As ordered. You see, princess, I did my research and made sure to order everything a British girl loves, and we have no need to leave these four walls until our ride home."

The fact the space is so small means she is always within reach and as she tries to shuffle back awkwardly, I feel the heat building between us and it's not because of the close confinement of the room.

I briefly wonder if it would help pass the time to corrupt this delectable English Rose, but always standing there like an avenging angel on her shoulder is the bastard she will call daddy from now on.

Tossing the box toward her, I say rudely, "Sort yourself out. I'll be entertaining my new best friend."

Grabbing the vodka, I leave her behind and head to my room. Luckily, we have two bedrooms, so it will give me some space and, as I lie on the bed and shift up against the pillows, I prepare myself for a very difficult stay.

CHAPTER 7

CHARLOTTE

*R*ussia is living up to every image I had of it so far, and none of it is good. The men are rough and angry, which matches the landscape perfectly. I'm still trying to get over the shock of being here at all and as I make the tea, I briefly consider making my captor a coffee because if he gets drunk, I may not be safe.

I see the expression in his eye before he guards it well. There's an interest there that should have me strapping every knife in this kitchen over my body. I've never been with a man before, but I've imagined it thousands of times while I read the pages of my latest romance novel, magazine story, or watched a scene from a film.

There is a morbid curiosity about the sins of the flesh and the girls at Rose Hall Academy speak about it with hushed whispers and nervous giggles. Some have tales to tell of an act that sounds so disgusting it made us gag. A horrifying pastime that shouldn't even be legal. But it is, and for some reason, I'm curious about that. Especially now, because my savage is the sexiest man I have ever met, and I have an overwhelming urge for just one taste.

The fact I also hate him pours cold water on my lustful thoughts and I can only hope that vodka does the trick and renders him unconscious before the night is out.

So, taking my chance, I explore the apartment and my heart sinks with every door opened when I see basic living in all its glory. It's almost as if they went to the local rubbish tip to furnish it and there's the strangest aroma I don't think I will ever get used to.

I start searching for clues as to my captor's identity so I can alert the police when I am returned home.

My phone is lost, probably when I was bundled into the car, so I have no communication with the outside world.

I just need to get a message to my father to tell him where I am, and he will send in the police to come and get me. Perhaps I can escape the apartment and find the local police station myself. They would help me, surely.

Feeling bold, I head toward the door we came in from and with a thumping heart, I grip the handle and turn. Then it sinks when the door stays firmly shut, revealing the savage has locked us in.

Turning, I glance across at the windows and note we are on the top floor, or at least it seems that way. It's definitely too high to jump and there isn't even a rusty fire escape outside to help me.

I am trapped in an apartment in, what did he call it, the most depressing city in the world and my only companion is probably under strict orders to kill me at a moment's notice.

A wry laugh escapes me when I remember that only a few hours ago I was praying for something good to happen. To live life on the edge. To be honest, this wasn't what I had in mind.

Resigned to it for now, I make the tea and almost groan as the caffeine hits my bloodstream and it's as if a little piece of home made it here with me.

As I sip the much needed pick me up I glance critically

around the depressing space. I don't even want to touch the settee with any part of my body, so decide to clean up this apartment at least.

Luckily, I find something that will do the job and set about my task more as a distraction than anything.

There is nothing here to provide any entertainment, no radio, no tv, or books, so I hum as I work, trying to bring sound to a deadly silent space.

"Why are you so happy?"

An angry growl startles me as I wipe down the windows and spinning around, I see the savage running his fingers through his scalp, apparently extremely pissed in every way.

"I'm British, you bastard. I make do and mend and try to make the best of a bad situation."

He snorts in derision and sinks down heavily on the couch.

"I suppose this is a day for firsts."

"What do you mean?"

"I'm guessing you don't clean much."

"I can clean." I stare at him with indignation, and he shrugs. "Cook then. I bet you have a chef to prepare your fancy meals."

"I can cook too." I stand facing him with my hands on my hips and scowl. "You think I'm some kind of pampered princess who can't care for herself. Well, breaking news, you kidnapped me from a frigging finishing school and what the fuck do you think they teach there?"

"How to swear, perhaps." He fires back and I curl my lip in disgust. "You bring out the bad-assed bitch in me, so deal with it."

He laughs out loud. "Don't you mean bad-arsed bitch? You are English, after all. Then again, perhaps we should re-title that the red-arsed bitch. I'm guessing yours is still dealing with the imprint of my hand."

"Do you want to fight me?"

I toss aside my cleaning spray and cloth and stand facing

him with a scowl on my face. "Because if you do, I am an expert in karate and taekwondo."

That gets his attention, and he looks up, a spark flaring in his eyes.

"You can fight?"

"I can. Care to try."

In a flash, he's on his feet and my mouth dries when I see the challenge in his eyes. Thinking back on my carefully constructed classes with our teacher, I'm not sure my skills are up to brawling at base level, but I'm willing to give it a go.

"OK."

He grins and advances slowly, standing before me with an amused grin.

"Take your shot."

I shrug out of my school blazer and rip off my tie and nod before bowing to him, as we have been taught to do.

His low laugh makes me bristle with anger and as I aim my first kick at his head, he steps aside and says in a bored voice, "Is that the best you can do?"

As I swing my body around, I take another aim and he catches hold of my ankle in his strong grasp, flipping me onto my back and sitting astride me, holding both of my hands above my head.

"You call that fighting." His lip curls and I bring my knee up and try to dislodge him, but he is heavier than me and merely laughs.

"You're pathetic and your teacher should be fired, because if that's the best they taught you, you fail."

He shifts off me and stares down with disappointment.

"For a moment there I thought we could amuse ourselves with the martial arts. Maybe you should go and bake a cake instead."

He turns his back, giving me the chance to scramble to my feet and aim a well-placed kick on the back of his knee. As he goes down, he hits the corner of the table with his head and his angry growl has me sprinting from the room. As I slam the bathroom door behind me, his angry yell as he thumps against it gives me a moment's respite before a huge crash makes me jump and nothing can save me from a very angry Russian who looks as if he wants to kill me.

I note the gash to his temple and the blood trickling down his face and experience a moment's guilt that I did that to him. Despite everything, the spanking aside, he hasn't hurt me, and this is how I've repaid him.

Reaching out, he grabs hold of my arms and twists them behind my back before dragging me from the room and forcing me down on to a wooden chair, where he binds my wrists behind my back before doing the same to my ankles.

As I scream and struggle, a broad hand lies flat against my mouth and he says roughly, "Scream and I'll cut your fucking tongue out."

Just the promise renders me speechless for life and as the tears pour down my face, I am now facing the consequences of my actions as he storms from the room, slamming the door behind him.

CHAPTER 8

IVAN

I'm not proud that I lost my temper. If anything, I feel like a fool and as I clean myself up, I note the shattered door falling on its hinges and growl with annoyance.

I let her get to me and demonstrated why I deserve every syllable of my name. I am a savage and it's never been any different.

Being the son of the most hated man in Russia, outside of the president, kind of makes you grow up fast. There was no love ever shown or father, son chats. Hell, I don't even know who my mother is and I'm guessing whoever she was, she is long gone now. Women don't last long in our world. They are there purely for entertainment value and as soon as they stop being a pleasant distraction, they are replaced by a new one.

Sighing, I press a pad against my face and try to stem the blood from a wound that's merely irritating rather than serious and think about the woman who is currently tied to a chair in the living room.

She doesn't deserve this treatment. She doesn't deserve this life and must be fucking terrified. One minute she's in some freaking school still in the Victorian era and the next thing she knows, she's sparring with a savage in the most depressing city in the world. It almost makes me laugh as I remember her challenge and the way she casually stood there and asked if I wanted a fight. The way she faced me down with her hands on her hips with all the fury of Hades flashing in her eyes piqued my interest.

It was a surprising switch from the domestic goddess cleaning the windows not moments earlier and that alone was surprising hearing her humming like a trapped bird in hell.

Now I've calmed down, I wonder if the cut affected me more than I first thought because I am a little nauseous. In fact, my reflection is starting to blur, and I wonder if I've got a concussion.

As I drop to my knees, I grip the side of the toilet basin and the bile rises in my throat, providing an overwhelming urge to be sick.

Something's wrong. I'm never sick and certainly not after a fight. I've been hit worse than this before, much worse and never been affected other than bruising and a few broken bones for my sins. Something definitely doesn't feel right and as I empty the contents of my stomach into the toilet, the dizziness hits me and an unwelcome thought hits me hard.

I've been poisoned.

I recognize the signs and as I hurl again, I remember back over the past twenty-four hours and the only thing I can put it down to is the warm waffles the flight attendant served to us on the plane.

Knowing I wasn't the only one who ate them, directs my thoughts to Charlotte and dragging my body to stand, I rinse out my mouth with the rather dubious water that flows from the taps.

As I lurch from the room, trying desperately to keep it together, I stagger into the living room and see an ashen face staring at me with fright.

"I'm going to be sick."

She gasps as she hangs her head and I nod, stumbling across to her chair and reaching for my knife.

Her head snaps up and she gasps, "What are you doing?"

I can't speak because the urge to hurl is too strong and mustering as much strength as I have left, I slice the bindings on her hands and feet and gasp, "Bathroom."

She slaps her hand across her mouth and nods, barely making the short distance before I hear her retching into the pan and my heart beats out of control as I struggle to make sense of this.

My internal organs feel as if they are being dragged from my body and I break out into a cold sweat as I reach for my phone.

I know the signs, and this isn't the result of E.coli. This is deliberate and I call the only man I can trust who answers immediately.

"Ivan."

"Malik." My voice is rough and dripping with torment and he says urgently, *"What happened?"*

"Poisoned."

I must give him credit because he speaks in a measured, controlled voice, without a hint of panic in it, and says firmly, *"If you survive, take the girl to the airfield. Steal a car if you must, but don't tell anyone. I'll send a plane."*

He cuts the call and I take a moment to get my breathing under control and take in some huge gulps of air. My stomach is churning, and my limbs are weak and I'm not even sure if I can walk, let alone make it from the apartment and steal a car. How long will it take Malik to send a plane, anyway? I'm doubtful he has one parked at the airfield and if I'm right, it will take several hours for it to land.

When I hear Charlotte retching down the hall, it reminds me I'm not alone in this and so I grab the side of the chair and haul myself up, the room spinning around me as I try to remain conscious.

My body is violently rejecting whatever has made its way into my system and I just pray I never digested enough of the poison to cause serious harm.

My mind returns to how hungry Charlotte was and the huge plate of food I left her with fills me with even more concern for her than myself and I stagger down the hallway and find her sprawled on the ground, her white face staring up at the ceiling with glassy eyes that appear as if they left life already.

Quickly, I run the tap and fill the glass with water and dropping to my knees, I lift her head and hold the glass to her lips. There is no reaction and so I gently trickle the liquid into her mouth and hold her head so it doesn't choke her.

"Wake up sleeping beauty." I say through ragged breaths, and she gags as the liquid hits the back of her throat, causing her to choke a little.

Her body reacts to the danger and brings her back and as she recovers, I say roughly, "Drink some more."

"I…" her voice sounds weak, and I snarl, "Drink it."

She drinks some more water and then I take a gulp myself and we must be a strange sight cowering on the small bathroom floor, seemingly knocking at death's door.

As her breathing speeds up, I say as if talking from a distance, "We must leave."

"I don't think…" her voice shakes and I say urgently, "We *must* leave. Can you stand?"

"I'll try."

As I grip the basin and haul my own large body to my feet, my head spins with the effort and I lean back against the wall, offering her my hand.

As hers closes around it, I hate the weakness in me as I try to help her to her feet.

Somehow, we manage it and without wasting any energy on words, I pull her along the hall with me and reach for the coats we discarded on the hook by the front door.

"We must run; this place is compromised."

She nods, looking as if she's about to hurl again but shrugs into the coat and attempts to help me with mine, causing me to smile a little. Despite everything, this small act of kindness hits me somewhere new, and as I stare at the pale beauty before me, I am strangely protective of her. That alone surprises me because I've only ever experienced that once before and it concerned my best friend's sister, Winter. I cared for her like the sister I never had and yet I already know what I'm feeling toward my pretty English rose isn't the love for a sister. It's something else entirely. Just that thought alone brings me round quicker than any medical solution and it's suddenly the most important thing in the world to get us both to safety.

CHAPTER 9

CHARLOTTE

This can't be happening to me. One minute I'm daydreaming in the English countryside and the next I'm in a strange dystopian city wondering if I'll make it out alive. To make matters worse, my kidnapper appears to be hovering close to death, and I'm not far behind him.

I can't remember ever being so ill in my life, and he doesn't seem much better and as I stagger after him back down the hated concrete staircase, I wonder what the fuck is going on.

As we exit, the cold wind makes me shiver but gives me some much-needed oxygen to inflate my wretched lungs and I'm surprised when he takes my hand and says roughly, "Stick close to me. I'm not sure if I'll get us there alive."

"What do you mean?"

My voice shakes as I sense danger approaching and he growls, "I'll tell you later. Trust me."

I would laugh out loud if I could but I'm so weak, I'm tempted to curl up and die in the stairwell of the slum I've just been evicted from.

As we set off, I wonder where we're going and why and as we turn the corner, the scene is a mirror image of the one we've left. Tall gray buildings that look as if they need tearing to the ground stand watching our progress with angry scowls. I'm certain nobody actually lives here because I haven't seen one human life form since I arrived.

I'm not even sure what time it is because the sky is gray and austere, much like when we arrived, and only the grit in my eyes reminds me I really should be sleeping by now.

I'm shocked when the savage heads toward what looks like a wrecked vehicle and removes a credit card from his pocket.

As the door flicks open, he says with an urgent whisper, "Hurry, we need to get on the road."

"Is this car yours?" I gasp in a hushed whisper, and he rolls his eyes. "Seriously, do you really think I'd buy this shit heap?"

"No." I shake my head.

"No, what?"

"I'm not stealing somebody's possession."

He almost growls with frustration, anger, or it could be a mixture of the two making me wonder about my sanity in standing up to him. Then without another word, he pushes me roughly into a car that smells as if something died in here and says hoarsely, "Do as I say if you want to live."

He jumps in beside me and I stare in astonishment as he proceeds to hot-wire the car and before I know it, we are screeching away from a place I never want to visit in my lifetime again.

The roads are in definite need of repair along with the entire city, if I'm honest, and if there was anything left inside me, it would surely be making an appearance round about now. As we speed off to God only knows where, I study my captor a little closer. He looks like shit, and I guess I'm not much better and I say with a hint of shock edging my words, "What's happening?"

"We've been poisoned."

I heard him right the first time, but say weakly, "That can't be right. Why would anyone want to poison us?"

"Welcome to Russia, moya krasivaya roza."

"What did you even say?"

He laughs softly, which is the first sign of normality in a man who makes a psychopath seem sane.

"I called you my pretty English rose."

"Oh." I'm surprised and yet it stirs a warm sensation inside me as I shrink back in my seat and let his endearment wash through my body like an antidote to a snake bite.

Just that one sentence makes me warm to him and then he surprises me again by saying sweetly, "How are you?"

"OK, I guess, under the circumstances."

His gruff laughter almost makes me smile and I say with curiosity, "What is your name, if I'm allowed to know such classified information?"

"Ivan."

His reply is short and sweet, and I roll it around in my mind.

For a moment I say nothing and then say tentatively, "You said we were poisoned. Who would do that?"

He sighs deeply and looks so tense it makes me afraid for our safety.

"It could be many people. I'm not sure who is responsible. So, for now, we must hide until we discover their identity."

"And the plan is…?"

I gently try to coax the information out of him, and he snaps, "There is no plan."

Well color me confused because now I'm even more worried and say urgently, "We should go to the British embassy. They will help us."

He laughs out loud, and I say tightly, "They will. What's so funny?"

"Even the British embassy can't protect us from whoever

this is. Do you really believe your government has any jurisdiction here? Do you imagine the American government has a magic wand hidden inside a frame on their marbled walls? No princess, this is mother fucking Russia, and she makes the rules up as she goes along. She's deadly, depraved and sly. She has no friends, and she trusts no one. She is the darkest demon dressed as an angel and would kill you dead with a welcoming smile. There are no friends in Russia and the fucking embassy is the last place we should go to for help."

"But you're Russian. Why are they trying to kill you?"

I'm a little stung by the derision in his voice and his laugh has no humor in it as he hisses, "Would it shock you to learn it may be my own father responsible?"

"Yes."

I gasp and he laughs bitterly. "It could also be yours. I'm still figuring that one out, though."

"Mine." Picturing my father being responsible for doing anything remotely like this seems preposterous and I say angrily, "My father may be an adulterer and easily led, but he's not a killer and why would he want to kill me? It doesn't make sense."

"I'm not talking about the man you call daddy, princess."

Like a knockout punch, his words hit home and wound me so deeply I'm winded for a second.

He must instantly regret his words because he reaches out and grasps my hand, which shocks me more than anything he just said.

"I'm sorry, Charlotte."

I blink in surprise because hearing my name on his lips is strange and before I can respond to that, he swerves down a track and says urgently, "This is the end of the road. We make the rest of the journey on foot. Can you walk?"

"I think so, but…"

"Then move."

He exits the car and curses as his feet hit the ground and once again, I wonder if he's ok himself. I haven't missed the angry cut on his head where he fell, and his ashen color tells me he's struggling as much as I am and as my own feet hit the ground, I know why because my legs are so weak, they almost buckle under me.

However, before I can fall, a strong hand grips mine and he says in a slightly warmer voice, "Come. We'll be safe soon enough, and then we can rest."

"But how will we be safe? Somebody is out to, well, get us."

Once again, he shakes his head and, sounding almost amused, whispers, "Like I said, trust me. I'll get you to safety even if the last thing I ever do."

He moves off as fast as his battered body will let him, and I swear I feel every stone under my shoe as my body struggles with unwanted activity. I notice we are hugging the perimeter of the airfield that we arrived at, and I see various planes waiting on the tarmac and wonder if, somehow, he intends to hot-wire one of those. I wouldn't put it past him and part of me is impressed by the warrior holding my hand so tenderly.

Ever since I met him, I've been fantasizing about him in a very inappropriate way. All it takes is one look at his strong jaw dusted with dark stubble and my legs go weak. The icy blue eyes that could cut glass and the close-cropped hair that is more practical than stylish tell me this man has more testosterone running through his veins than blood.

I like it–a lot and he intrigues me. Our conversations have been brief and I long to tear away a little more of the packaging because I have a feeling that what's inside is a rare find for a woman like me.

CHAPTER 10

IVAN

I don't understand how she is still walking because I'm on my last breath and my muscles deserted me somewhere between the apartment and arriving here. I am desperate to survive just to keep her safe. The thought of this being the end for both of us in this god forbidden hell hole, spurs me on even further.

I will make my mission count and I won't let Club Mafia down, but for every minute I spend in Charlotte Richmond's company, a little piece of my spirit dies inside. I can't shake the image of her future. The man she is heading to and will soon call daddy. The fact I will be instrumental in sending her to hell is not sitting well with me and yet she is the key to the lock of Winter's prison. Without her, we won't get our sister back but something is making me hold back a little. I'm not sure I can see this through because the last thing this woman deserves is what fate has in store for her.

"Ivan." Her soft voice disturbs my dark thoughts and I stop, turning to face the object of them.

"What?" Her white pinched face causes me concern as the

dark shadows underneath her eyes tell me she needs sleep as much as I do.

"I'm worried about you."

Her words cause more damage than the poison currently searing through my veins, and I hitch my breath at this unexpected situation.

She peers at me with concern and just the fatigue in her eyes and the slight tremble to her lip causes something to shift inside me. Since when did emotion play a place in my life?

Never, for a very good reason.

I don't form attachments and if I do, the only ones I have are with men like me. Not women. Winter is different, she's family. I'm not thinking of Charlotte in that way for sure and yet I only enjoy a woman's company for one night only. That's the rule I live by and can be the only rational explanation why I'm struggling now. She's becoming too familiar, and I need to cut off the snake's head before it bites, so I say sharply, "You have no business being concerned about me. Now shut the fuck up and keep quiet before I gag you."

I turn away feeling like a shitty bastard, but I am doing this for both our sakes. Despite the situation we're in we need to maintain distance and I am drawing the line and erecting the wall because I will not let any feelings for this woman take root.

* * *

WE REACH the edge of the airfield and I pull her behind a tree that shields us but gives us the perfect view of any approaching aircraft.

With my back to the tree, I pull her down to sit between my legs and as my arms wrap around her shivering body, I push the emotion away.

"We could be some time." I say harshly. "Get some sleep and I'll keep watch."

She says nothing, which upsets me more than I thought it would, even though I threatened to gag her if she spoke. I am seriously losing my mind right now and blame it on the poison in my bloodstream. I really need to shrug this mood off and reclaim control of my life if we are going to make it back to civilization alive.

As we sit like Hansel and Gretel in the forest, I'm happy when she leans back against my chest and her even breathing tells me she's fallen asleep. It's strangely comforting as I hold her in my arms, loving the warmth she provides and knowing I'm not on my own.

It strikes me I'm always on my own, unless you count the women I fuck for pleasure and nothing more.

But this is different. I have an actual life in my calloused hands, and I'm surprised to find I'm enjoying every minute of it.

I even catch myself brushing my lips against the top of her hair and breathing in the scent of a woman. She feels so soft, delicate even, and like Adam's apple, is the most forbidden fruit.

She stirs and her soft moan escapes into the air and just hearing the gentle sound makes me tighten my grip a little. It's as if I'm holding a newly born baby, and the protective surge she has created shocks me a little.

I am tempted to close my eyes and give into the darkness myself, but only my will to survive this nightmare keeps me alert.

My darkest thoughts are my only companion as I try to figure out who wants us both dead. As I play with the possibilities, nothing adds up.

Was I the intended target and, because I shared my food with Charlotte, I dragged her into it?

Could it have been my men on board that plane eager to get me out of the way, but for what? They would never go against my father unless the bastard himself ordered the hit.

Perhaps he discovered who my precious cargo really is, and my tale of kidnap and ransom was revealed as a lie. I know my father hates Massimo Delauren as much as the rest of us, but I understand it's always business with him. If Massimo somehow discovered it was the bratva who snatched his daughter away before he could reach her, it would explain his deal with my father. But why risk harming her? That also doesn't make sense.

The fact they knew we would be holed up in Norilsk waiting for the signal tells me they intended for us to die there. Either from the poison or from an assassin being sent to finish the job. That was why we ran. Malik was right to order it and I hope to God he has a plan to get us to safety because Club Mafia are the only ones I trust right now, knowing they are the only people who have my back without sticking a knife in it.

The hard ground and the temperature are not helping, especially as I dare not move out of fear of waking the sleeping beauty in my arms. It's only my devious thoughts keeping me awake right now and I'm not sure how long we have been in this position before I hear a plane coming into land.

My heart rate increases as I watch it touch down and taxi to the most remote part of the airfield. Then I watch the lights flash three times and know this is our ride out of here and, leaning down, I whisper, "Baby, wake up."

With a start she jumps, and I whisper, "Follow me. We must remain in the shadows."

I can only imagine it's the adrenalin that kick starts us into action and as we circle the perimeter under the cover of trees, it doesn't take long before we reach the plane.

Thanking God, Norilsk is such a shit show, I use my knife

to enlarge a hole in the wire fencing, enabling us to crawl through.

The door to the aircraft opens and I hold my breath as I drag Charlotte in one hand and raise my gun in the other and as the steps lower and a man in uniform peers out, I see the livery of Malik's family emblazoned on his jacket and breathe a sigh of relief.

I think we break all records for boarding an aircraft and as the steps fold up behind us, we fall into the luxurious jet belonging to Malik's Arab family.

"Welcome on board Mr. Volkov. Miss. Richmond."

The captain nods respectfully and says quickly, "Please take your seats. We need to be airborne inside of five minutes."

Realizing I still have hold of Charlotte's hand, I guide her to the nearest seat and quickly strap her in like a child before taking the one next to her.

As the plane's engine starts up, I look out of the window and notice some headlights heading our way and pray this captain knows what he's doing because if I'm not mistaken, those cars are here for us.

CHAPTER 11

CHARLOTTE

He told me not to speak, and the bastard had better get used to it because why am I even bothering? He was so rude, and it wounded my already battered pride still further and I sit bristling beside him with the anger pushing aside any fear I have for my own safety.

Fucking savage is the best name for him and I can only imagine he received it from a past girlfriend. Imagining the torture he must have put her through makes me hope she dumped him, and it hurt badly. That can be the only explanation for his rude misogyny and as soon as we reach wherever we're going, I am going to put in place an escape plan I have yet to formulate in my mind.

As the plane starts moving, I am full of dark thoughts toward my captor, which includes strangling him with the lifejacket cord under my seat if I get the opportunity.

To think I was concerned for him. Well, that won't happen again and suddenly a loud bang makes me jump and before I know what's happening, he grabs the back of my neck and pushes me face down toward the floor, yelling, "Keep low and away from the windows."

Immediately forgetting I'm not speaking to him, I yell, "What the fuck is happening?"

"They've found us."

"Who? The police?"

I'm almost hoping that's the case, but his derisive laugh causes me to hate him all over again.

"The fucking bastards who want us dead, so if you want to live to irritate me some more, shut the fuck up and keep your head down."

Now I'm afraid because that sounds like gunfire and it hasn't escaped my notice that we are sitting on an unexploded bomb with all the fuel in our tanks and as the plane increases its speed, I almost expect to meet my maker in a blaze of glory.

Maybe the fact my life is flashing before my eyes confuses my already scrambled brain because I reach for Ivan's fingers and clasp them so tightly, whispering, "If we don't make it, thank you for trying to save me."

The way he is crushing my hand causes me to wince as he growls, "We will die another day, malyshka. Today is not that day."

As the plane lifts off from the ground, I hold my breath and count to ten and as we soar high into the air, my heart provides the fuel because I have never been so high on adrenalin in my life.

By the time the plane levels out and the engines stop screaming, I open my eyes and take a deep sigh of relief. So far, so good.

Ivan drags my hand with him and clutches it tightly as he exhales sharply and, to my surprise, lifts my hand and brushes his lips against it, closing his eyes, looking more relieved than anything.

As I glance down at the ink on his fingers that are brutally different to my own manicured ones, it makes me shiver a little inside. Images of what he could do with those hands to bring me pleasure make me weak, and this time it's not because of the poison inside me. It's him. He is the poison that corrupted me because I shouldn't want him. I shouldn't even like him, and I shouldn't be infatuated with him because he is the man responsible for tearing my world apart.

I glance up as the door to the cockpit opens, and the pilot heads out, briefly causing me alarm as I question who is flying this freaking plane and he catches the fear on my face and smiles with amusement.

"It's ok, my co-pilot has taken over."

I sigh with relief as he sits opposite and stares at us with concern.

"Mr. Karim has instructed us to fly you to Poland, where a connecting flight will take you to Switzerland. A helicopter will transport you to his home where you will wait for further instructions."

I stare at him in complete surprise and glance down at my rather dirty uniform and know it must appear as if I died already. Ivan is no better in his battered combats and sweater, and there's also the part where we have no personal documentation.

I keep my mouth shut though because I haven't forgotten his rudeness earlier, and suddenly all my questions are answered as the captain removes a manila envelope from a storage compartment and hands it to Ivan.

"Your papers are in here with new identities. Mr. Karim has arranged a change of clothing that you will find in the cabin at the rear of the aircraft. I would advise showering and grabbing something to eat. Flight time will be roughly five hours, so you may want to get some sleep."

"Have you any other passengers?" Ivan's voice is gruff, and I'm surprised at the question because I thought we were alone, and the captain shakes his head.

"No crew as requested by Mr. Karim. We have registered

you both as passengers under your new names and there is no record of you being here at all under your original ones."

"Good." Ivan fixes him with a harsh glare, and I feel bad for the captain, so I smile softly and say, "Thank you so much."

His soft gaze makes me almost want to curl up in his arms and tell him to save me, which obviously doesn't go unnoticed by Ivan, who growls, "Thank you. We will be in our cabin."

I think I'm more shocked than the captain when Ivan fixes him with a dark look, promising all manner of horrors and positively drags me behind him toward the rear of the aircraft.

Now my heart is thumping for an entirely different reason because he said *our* cabin. What the fuck is he implying here?

I follow him through a door and blink in astonishment at the luxurious room that looks completely out of place on an aircraft.

"Ivan." My voice sounds hushed and far away as I whisper, "I'm hallucinating again."

His low laugh takes me by surprise, and he chuckles. "My friend has more money than God. This is one of his smaller toys."

I blink as I gaze around at an actual bedroom. Dressed in black silk sheets and fur throws is a frigging king-sized bed with drapes hanging heavy on the side. Cream leather chairs sit either side of a porthole and the white shag pile carpet looks brand new. Gold mirrors and chandeliers dress the room in the finest luxury, and I blink again as Ivan pulls me into what appears to be a dressing room, leading on to a full-sized bathroom.

I watch in disbelief as he turns on the tap and seizes a bottle of foaming oil and pours a generous amount into it and my mouth dries as he rips off his sweater and I almost pass out at the bare chest flexing before my eyes. I can't stop staring and not because it is covered completely in ink. It's almost tribal and the muscles and well-defined abs make me lose my mind.

A low laugh makes me raise my eyes and his eyes shine with mischief as he smirks. "Like what you see, princess?"

"Not really." I turn away and try to get my breathing under control because I am the biggest, fattest liar in the world right now.

I *love* what I see. I could stare at it all night and all day if I had to. How is this man even real, for Christ's sake?

As I look back, I almost wish I hadn't because now the combats have joined the sweater on the floor, and it appears underwear is not required.

I quickly spin around and hiss, "For fuck's sake, don't you have any manners?"

"No."

His low laugh makes the blood rise in my face as I blush furiously and I actually whimper when he says with amusement, "What's taking you so long?"

"What do you mean?" I face the other way and he laughs. "I thought you'd be glad to rid yourself of that uniform. Come on baby, don't be shy. Haven't you seen a man naked before?"

I squeeze my eyes tightly shut and whisper, "No."

The silence returns and I swallow hard and then I almost jump out of my skin when a rough hand touches my shoulders and a softer voice says, "Turn around, malyshka."

"No."

I'm actually shaking and yet he won't give in and spins me around to face him and lifts my chin, so I'm staring into those stunning eyes and I almost whimper when he says softly, "Relax, I'm not going to hurt you. We need to clean up and change, and that's all this is. If it helps, you take the bath and I'll take the shower."

"Can't I do it in private?" I run my tongue over my dry lips, and he shakes his head slowly, an evil grin lighting up his features, making me speechless for a moment.

"I don't want to let you out of my sight for a second."

"But we're thirty thousand feet in the air! Where do you think I'll go? Or is there a docking station through that door leading to an escape pod, where I will man the controls and head back to England in time for afternoon tea on the lawn?"

Even I start to laugh as his face breaks out into a broad smile and his laughter lightens the atmosphere for a minute before I'm shocked into silence when his lips brush against mine and he whispers, "Because it would break my heart if anything happened to you."

I blink in astonishment because where has this come from and as his lips hover dangerously close to mine, I almost think he's going to kiss me. I actually hope he is because the tension that's been building between us needs dealing with, but now is obviously not that time because he closes his eyes and sighs deeply. "Don't fight me, Charlotte. Remember, you're my prisoner and just so you know, your fighting skills could use some serious work."

Once again, he grins, and I am so confused right now. Then he strokes my face like a pet dog and the emotion in his eyes takes me by surprise as he says softly, "I promise I won't look. I'll take the shower and if you face away from me, the bubbles will cover your modesty."

Realizing I don't have a choice, I nod slowly and step back and as his hands drop away from me, I feel the loss already. Then, as he turns and walks over to the shower, I can't help checking out his ass as he goes.

CHAPTER 12

IVAN

I am officially fucked, and not in the usual way. It took all my self-control not to push things with Charlotte. I want her. More than I've wanted anyone, and I'm guessing it's because she's here. I have never spent so long with a girl before and certainly not one that intrigues me as much as this one does. It's taking a superhuman effort not to test the water and dive straight in. I know she's a virgin. Just the embarrassment on her face and the yearning mixed with curiosity in those beautiful eyes tells me that. She almost whimpered when she saw my naked body and I'm sure if I pushed things, she would be in my arms willingly by now.

But the entire time, this mission is controlling me and reminding me she's not mine to enjoy. She is my angel to sacrifice, and I must remember the stakes are high.

As the warm jets cleanse the dirt away, I wish it could do the same with my mind. It's raging with possibilities right now about what I want to do to the English rose currently taking a dip in a gold–plated tub.

Fuck Malik and his family. They make my own seem like trailer trash. I have never seen luxury quite like this and I'm as impressed as Charlotte obviously is. When I saw the huge fucking bed dressed for sin, beckoning me inside, all I could think of was how good her naked body would look writhing in those sheets with my cock buried deep inside her and making her scream.

My cock throbs in agony as I pump it hard because fuck me, this is worse than any torture her psychotic father could conjure up.

I release a steady stream of cum to the floor and watch it escape through the drain and it brings with it a certain sense of release. As I soap my body and shampoo my hair, I try to wrestle my turbulent thoughts under control. However, it's impossible to do all the time the object of those thoughts is naked on the other side of this screen, relaxing in a deep filled bath of decadent luxury.

This room has all the trappings of a lover's paradise, and I must endure the most exquisite torture with a woman I am interested in way too much for my own good.

Making sure to give her enough time, I exit the shower and am not surprised to find her wrapped in a silk robe, her hair wet with droplets of water sliding down her face.

It's just too much and the slight tremble to her lip and the flush to her cheeks are like a powerful magnet as they draw me to her side in a second. As I stand unsure before her, I sense a shift coming that spells trouble for everyone.

To my surprise, she reaches out and touches my chest. "I love your tattoos."

Such a simple statement that fills me with pride and she points to a dark looking script that lies just above my chest. "What does that mean?"

I look down and say roughly, "It's Russian for a savage heart."

As her fingers graze my skin, it's like the purest torture and she points to another. "And this one?"

She points to a bird in a cage, and I say, "Freedom."

"But the bird is caged."

She looks up, and I wince when I see the lust sparkling in her obscenely beautiful eyes.

"It's a promise of freedom. One day, I will have another image inked to my skin of the cage door open and the bird on the other side."

"You're talking about you, aren't you, Ivan?"

She looks at me with so much sadness and it hurts like hell knowing she's right. I hate the fact my voice is weaker than normal when I hold her hand against my skin and whisper, "My body is my canvas. It scripts my journey and tells my story to the world. An open book if you like that only I understand the meaning of. One day the story inked on my skin will be a very different one and that is what gets me through the madness."

She nods and circles a clear patch of skin. "What will you put there?"

I don't even hesitate. "A beautiful rose."

She stares up at me in startled surprise and shifts a little closer, her hand reaching behind my neck as she whispers, "Can I ask you for something, Ivan?"

I doubt I can deny her anything right now and I nod before she says hesitantly, "Please, may I steal a kiss?"

She looks worried and the slight break in her voice makes me burn inside and reaching up, I cup both her cheeks in my rough hands and whisper, "Anything for you, princess."

Our lips connect and as I enjoy my first taste of this woman, I lose every last shred of gallantry I had. She tastes so sweet like I always knew she would and as I suck her lower lip into my mouth and bite down gently on the plump cushion, my cock throbs so hard it physically hurts.

My tongue claims hers and her low moan encourages me in deeper, and as I hold her in my arms, it is possibly the most beautiful moment of my life. She is so innocent. A beautiful angel who has somehow survived what life has thrown at her and approached it with unwavering bravery and curiosity. This is no exception and as her hands lay flat against my chest and she kisses me back, I don't think I have ever been happier in my life.

As I pull away, I rest my head against hers and whisper, "Thank you."

"I should be the one thanking you."

The light amusement in her voice makes me smile and as I make to pull away, I'm surprised when she pulls me back and says with a sigh. "Can I ask you another favor, please?"

My breath hitches as I nod slowly. "Of course."

"Will you sleep with me, Ivan?"

I stare at her in surprise, and she blushes furiously. "I mean, not like that, it's just, well, I only feel safe when I'm with you and I'm so tired I don't think I can keep my eyes open for another second."

With a small smile, I nod. "Of course. Come, we could both use some sleep."

It's strange slipping naked in between the black silk sheets with a woman dressed in a silk robe. I can feel the warm heat from her body as the fabric caresses it and molds her curves. I physically ache to run my hands down the length of her and plunge my fingers inside to touch her sticky wet heat. I know it's there but is locked away for someone else to discover. Not me. Not the bastard who took her to hell and almost took up permanent residency there. I need to be better for once in my life and do what she's asking. Protect her because God knows, there is one thing I can never protect her from and that is the madness heading our way that goes by the name Massimo Delauren.

CHAPTER 13

CHARLOTTE

I must have fallen into a blissful sleep courtesy of the warm bath, sensual oils and the deep soul shattering kiss of a god. Ivan is a god to me. Somehow, he has gone from being an aggressor, a kidnapper and a bastard, to becoming an object of fascination. He intrigues me, and not just because I'm inexperienced. It's him. The savage warrior who is keeping me alive right now, and that alone is a powerful aphrodisiac.

As I lie in his arms wrapped in decadence, it's a world away from the depressing place we've just left. My life has become a movie and I'm starring in the role of a lifetime with a savage as my leading man. I never thought this would happen to a girl like me, but now it has I'm keen to explore every inch of insanity I possess because I know when this ends, I will never be the same again.

Waking up beside Ivan is blissful agony. It feels so good with his legs entwined in mine. His rough hand grazing my stomach as his arm traps me beneath tribal ink. His breath fans my face and I steal a glance at the most beautiful man I have ever seen. He could star in every action movie I have ever seen, and I couldn't desire him more. I'm not even embarrassed that he's naked against my silk covered body. I like it, which makes me curious.

He stirs and my heart thumps as he opens one bright blue eye and grins, his lazy smile dragging my own shy one onto my face.

"This is better."

I nod, suddenly shy for no apparent reason.

To my surprise, he regards me with a curious expression that makes my heart race, and his hand tightens against my thigh. I can't help myself and inch even closer and his low groan of frustration matches what I'm thinking.

Then, to my extreme disappointment, he rolls to the side and exhales sharply. "We should dress. You need to eat, and pray this time it's not with any unwelcome added ingredients.

The disappointment hits me hard as our cozy bubble bursts and lets reality in.

Sighing, I swing my legs to the side of the bed, not even caring that the robe falls off one shoulder, revealing a glimpse of flesh that Ivan obviously doesn't appreciate because he snaps, "For fuck's sake, let's see what clothes my friend has packed before I do something we'll both regret. He stomps into the dressing room and returns with two black bags and chucks them onto the bed.

As I unzip one of them, I pull out a smart dress and some matching heels, loving how luxurious the material feels against my touch. "Your friend has good taste."

I hold up the lacey lingerie and Ivan sucks in a breath, making me giggle at his tortured expression.

"Fuck! Now I'm stuck with an image of you wearing that as we head to whatever madness waits for us."

He groans, and it makes me laugh and then he removes a black suit and a smart black silk shirt from his own bag, making my own mouth water. "A dangerous outfit for a dangerous man." I say slyly, and he rolls his eyes.

"I've never heard a fucking suit described as dangerous before. You're one screwed up woman."

His chuckle makes me smile and I'm not sure what madness grips my reasoning, but I shrug and slip the robe from my body, not caring that I'm as naked as he is.

His low 'fuck' makes me shiver with delight as I reach for the silky vest and pull it over my head. The matching knickers, or panties, as he calls them, follow and I pointedly ignore the fact he is just standing watching as if in a trance.

After I shrug on the black dress, I step into the killer heels and marvel that they fit at all.

Ivan is still staring and the look in his eye should make me run for cover because it's obvious what he wants. *Me.*

Sitting back on the bed, I say casually, "What are you waiting for?"

He turns abruptly and dresses in record speed, and now it's my turn to stare in stunned surprise. He scrubs up well, and the savage is almost respectable as he becomes the man I know he is most of the time. Mafia, Bratva, it's one and the same and this man exudes danger, which is like a love potion of the most devastating kind.

As he holds out his hand, my own finds it willingly, almost as if it was made to fit like Cinderella's glass slipper and as we leave the most amazing and surprising room I have ever seen, two very different people step outside.

We help ourselves to the food in the small galley and I'm grateful to find fresh fruit and English muffins are in plentiful supply. There's even a toaster and English butter and as I help myself, I make enough for the two of us along with a coffee for Ivan and my desired English tea. We dine at a table that could seat at least twelve and I gaze around me in wonder.

"Do people really live like this?"

"It appears they do."

"Tell me about your friend." I'm curious about the man who has rescued us from certain death, and Ivan shrugs. "We met at college and shared a house with three other guys. Malik is from Dubai and his father is the security advisor to the Sheikh. I almost think they print money in their many palaces because I have never known living like this."

"Do you trust him?"

I'm curious about that and hope he can because if he's in on this, we could be walking into an ambush anytime soon.

"With my life."

Ivan looks determined about that and says in a low voice, "We are blood brothers. There were six of us who swore an oath on the last day of college. Paid for in blood."

"Blood!" The horror must show on my face because he grins, and it's as if the devil has entered the room.

"We cut our skin and signed our names in blood and that bond will never be broken."

"Wow." I can't get my head around this. "It's like something out of a freaking book. What was your oath?"

"To turn our backs on love and remove our hearts. To free Angelo's sister from a maniac and bring her back to us."

"His sister?"

I'm confused and Ivan shakes his head, appearing quite sad. "Winter came to live with us at Rockwell Academy in our last semester. Angelo is her twin brother, and they lived the same life we all did. She was being married off after graduation to someone of her father's choosing and she was afraid."

"I'm not surprised. Who wants an arranged marriage?"

"Definitely not when the man is old enough to be your father and is the biggest bastard mafia boss in the world."

"That's disgusting." I feel sick and Ivan growls. "Anyway, I don't want to talk about it."

He looks down and I'm a little surprised because something has slammed the door shut and I feel a pang when I think of the reason. It must be Winter. He must love her and it's tearing him up, thinking of her with another man. For some reason, my appetite deserts me and I push my plate away and stare out at the clouds below us.

"You're not eating." His gruff voice brings my attention back to him and I force a bright smile onto my face.

"I've had enough. Thank you."

He stares at me long and hard and then shakes his head. "Are you always so polite?"

"Of course, manners cost nothing despite the circumstances."

He chuckles, which makes me smile. "What?"

"You. My perfect little English rose looking as if she's taking tea with the queen, not the Russian bastard who kidnapped her and nearly got her killed."

"Yes, well, some things can't be helped, and you have to make the best of a bad situation."

"Is that what this is, a bad situation?"

For some reason, he looks a little disappointed and I shrug. "I suppose it is, but it has its good points."

"Is that so." He laughs and looks me straight in the eye which makes me shiver with lust because quite frankly I think I'm heading down some kind of crazy highway with this handsome Russian that will only end up in one place—his bed.

"If you must know, the company isn't as bad as I expected."

"Is that right?"

"Yes, although I would have preferred more of a challenge."

"In what way?"

He seems amused, and I lean forward and smile suggestively. "I had hoped he could teach me to be a better fighter, among other things."

"Other things." He cocks his brow and I shrug.

"Yes. Other things."

"What are they?" The smirk on his face makes me smile

because I love this easy relationship we're building and, feeling bolder, I sigh. "It's no fun being me, Ivan."

"I'm crying for you, princess." He rolls his eyes as I shrug.

"You think my life is easy and compared to yours, it is. However, like your friend's twin, my life is already mapped out for me."

"I'm still not buying it, baby."

"Well, think about it. I was sent off to boarding school for most of my life and some may say I've done a life sentence already. There is no freedom in an English school, not for the wealthy, anyway. I am locked away with girls like me and kept separate from boys for our own protection. We are taught what it's like to be a good wife and mother and how to charm the most suitable husband we can hook on our line."

"Still not crying."

He leans back and takes a sip of his coffee, and I sigh theatrically. "When I asked you to kiss me, it was the boldest question I had ever asked because as it happens, that was my first kiss—ever."

Now I have his attention and he seems shocked. "Ever!"

"Yes. I told you I have lived with girls my entire life and even when the holidays came around, they were spent in tennis club, cookery school, or deep in the countryside in my parent's country home. Strictly no boys allowed and every move I made was watched."

"So, you've never had a boyfriend."

Ivan looks curious, and I nod. "You're catching on. Anyway, the day you kidnapped me, I prayed hard for a different life. Something cool and edgy and it appears my wish was granted."

"You wanted this." He laughs as if I've cracked the funniest joke and I nod. "I want life, Ivan. I want to love, laugh, and live. I want freedom and not to live by the rule book. Kissing you was the single best experience of my life so far and to you, it was probably one in a very long line. I just want you to know that because, despite the circumstances, at least you have given me something to treasure in my boring future married to a wet blanket."

"A what?"

He looks confused and I laugh out loud. "It's a term we use like a wet weekend. Someone boring, plain, and unimaginative. Going through the motions of life rather than living it. I am now open to receiving your pity. Thank you."

He sets down his cup and stares deeply into my eyes.

"My story is a much better one."

"I'll be the judge of that."

This time I raise my cup and take a sip of the tea that feels a lot like home.

"I never knew my mother. Only a father whose idea of raising his son was making him fight. Ever since I can remember, he entered me in contests against local kids and if I didn't paint them in their own blood, he took mine instead."

The cup freezes against my mouth as he says dully. "I lost my virginity with my father's girlfriend while he watched."

Now I put the cup down and wish I had never asked. "I was fourteen years old."

I reach out and take his hand and as his fingers lace with mine, he says roughly, "I was educated in the school of life and dragged around after him as he tortured, murdered and raped his victims. I was encouraged to participate and the only time I ever earned his approval was when I won a fight."

It's as if he's speaking of somebody else because there is no emotion in his voice at all and he says with a sigh. "Fighting became my safety blanket. If I won, he was happy, which made me happy. I sought his approval because he was the big bad monster everybody feared. I grew to love what I did. For every bone I broke, I was rewarded. I had everything. Women, food, and alcohol. An unlimited expense account and no rules but one. To win."

He breaks off and I see the light dancing in his eyes as he says with a smile. "His biggest mistake was sending me to America to be educated. The place was called Rockwell Academy, and I met my future there. Along with my friends, we will change our future and live our lives the way we want to and not how our families have planned. Like you, I want a different life to the one mapped out for me and kidnapping you will give us everything we want."

"How?" I hold my breath because I wasn't expecting this, and he says darkly, "I lied about the reason I kidnapped you."

"You did." Now I'm afraid because the conversation has a darker edge to it, and he nods, looking at me with a tortured expression.

"As it turns out, Winter's husband wants to trade."

He appears disgusted as he spits, "We exchange you both and everyone gets what they want."

"Everyone." I feel weak and desperate as I face the real reason I'm here, and he nods.

"Massimo Delauren, as it turns out, is your biological father."

CHAPTER 14

IVAN

I feel like the biggest bastard in the world as I watch Charlotte's life crashing and burning at her feet. Her expression says it all as I lay out the real reason behind this.

She looks shocked and yet we can't talk about it because the captain calls me and tells us we'll be landing shortly.

As we clear and stow away the breakfast things, I sit beside a shocked Charlotte as we wait to land.

Since hearing she has a different father to the one she calls daddy, she has been as silent as a person who was born without a voice.

I should be worried about her, but I was cruel for a reason. Whatever is building between us must stop, because I have to give her up. It was never an option to form an attachment and there are more than my emotions riding on this. It's my brothers and Winter and I must put them first, before me, before her, before us.

As we land, I reach for the envelope and pull out the necessary paperwork and see two airline tickets accompanied by new passports. There is a credit card and a driving license, and it appears that Malik has thought of everything.

The plane taxis to a stop and still Charlotte says nothing and as the door opens and the customs officer step on board, I hand over our paperwork, hoping to God they don't question us.

The officer looks at the paperwork and his eyes slide over Charlotte, and I don't miss the appreciative glance he throws her, which makes me uncharacteristically jealous. I know she's hot and looking like a million dollars and even with no make-up, I have never seen a more natural beauty in my life.

"Mrs. Belton." She looks up and smiles, her perfect English manners serving her well on this occasion.

"Yes."

You would never believe anything was wrong, as she bats her lashes and smiles adorably. "I'm pleased to meet you."

I can tell the officer is won over already, and he nods and smiles before turning his attention to me. This time his expression is a very different one as he says coolly, "Your connecting flight to Switzerland is waiting. The last passengers have boarded, and they need to leave in the next five minutes. Do you have any luggage?"

"It's fine. We can pick up what we need when we get there."

He nods and then flashes another smile at Charlotte before saying respectfully, "If you would like to follow me, I'll make sure you get there on time."

Nodding my thanks to the captain and watching Charlotte hug him accompanied by a warm smile, I shake my head, suddenly annoyed for some reason, and follow behind as she chatters sweetly with the officer. She pointedly ignores me and for some reason I don't like it one bit, and I briefly wonder why she hasn't alerted him to her situation. That thought alone keeps me going because I'm holding onto the one last shred of hope I have that maybe, just maybe, I can make both our futures a little different somehow.

* * *

WE MAKE it to the commercial aircraft barely on time and as the doors close behind us, we are shown to two seats in first class. Charlotte is sitting in the one in front of me, which means I can always keep my eye on her. I didn't miss the curious looks of the passengers as we entered the cabin, and I'm guessing we appear a little out of place dressed in our formal wear as if we're about to head up a board meeting. The fact I look exactly what I am doesn't help with my dark black suit and menacing vibe, which definitely has a few people on edge.

Charlotte, however, wafts through the cabin like a summer breeze and smiles sweetly at anyone who looks her way, and an ache somewhere deep inside me is starting to grow whenever I study her. I'm not used to being around women for lengthy periods of time, and my attachment to her is growing. For some reason, I am starting to care, which is definitely not a good thing.

As the flight takes off, I begin to relax because there was a part of me that was uneasy. Any official could have stopped the plane and removed us, and I wouldn't put it past Massimo to add airport officials to his pay list. I know he won't be far behind me and it's making me edgy. Charlotte is now his number one priority and, according to Flynn, he will stop at nothing to bring her home to him.

Angelo told me the story behind why Charlotte ended up in England and hearing that Massimo never knew she existed is a sad story of loss and pain. However, they did Charlotte a huge favor because until now, she has led a much better life than the one she would have. I'm guessing that's why I'm uneasy about this. The fact we are using her to save Winter is not sitting well with me, and I wonder what I can do about that.

Halfway through the flight, I look up to find Charlotte standing beside my seat and leaning down, hisses, "Your friend has a fucking twisted sense of humor."

She waves her passport in my face, causing me to smirk. "Blame him, not me."

"I can't believe he did that. I am mortified beyond belief."

I can't help laughing and notice a few of the passengers around us are looking on with curiosity and feeling devilish, I reach out and drag her ass down onto my lap, whispering, "Perhaps it was a message to me."

"Whatever it was, it isn't funny, and how will I be able to look the passport officer in the face? He will think this is a joke and I'll be arrested."

As I run my hand around the back of her head, I pull her lips to mine and whisper, "I thought that was what you wanted. The police will save you, won't they?"

The fact we're in such a confined space means the heat from her body is radiating against mine and I bury my face against her sweet-smelling skin. Just holding her on my lap is causing me serious discomfort, and I am going through the purest torture right now.

"People are watching." She hisses and I whisper, "Then we should give them something to look at."

I can't help myself and claim those tempting lips and kiss her deep and hard, loving how her body relaxes against mine and her fingers rake through my hair as she gives back as good as she gets.

"Um, sir…"

We break apart and it amuses me to see the blushing face of the flight attendant as she stands holding the tray of food I ordered.

"I'm well, sorry, but your meal is ready."

Charlotte, to her credit, just smiles sweetly and says in that clipped British accent I am beginning to love hearing, "Of course, I'm so sorry. Please forgive us."

She grins at the flight attendant who smiles back with a mixture of jealousy and admiration and as Charlotte takes her seat and waits for her own meal, I try to distance my mind from how crazy she makes me when I'm around her.

CHAPTER 15

CHARLOTTE

I groan inwardly as I replace the passport in the purse Ivan's friend provided. Chastity Belton. How was that a good idea? Everything looks genuine enough on the passport, even my photograph, which makes me wonder about these men. How has he managed to whip up a fake passport in almost no time and it actually worked? The last customs officer didn't seem at all bothered by it, and I am cringing inside when I picture the laugh they must be having right now at this frigging stupid name. Ivan didn't help either. It's ok for him, he isn't going to be a subject of ridicule in the customs officers' staff room later when they laugh and joke about the woman with the very unfortunate sounding name.

However, when Ivan mentioned the police, it struck a chord because suddenly getting away from him isn't as attractive as it was a couple of days ago. In fact, when he dragged me onto his knee and kissed me so deeply, I loved every second of it. He makes my head spin, and my principles desert me in a heartbeat because around him, it's as if I'm living my life and not merely going through the motions.

The stewardess delivers my own meal and I smile and say a

polite thank you and love seeing the admiration in her eyes. I know we make a striking couple. It's obvious from the lingering looks of the ladies when Ivan walks past and the admiration on the faces of the men. I've caught the man across the aisle from me looking a few times already and for once, I feel so good about myself. Dressed in the sexiest lingerie and wearing a designer dress, is enough to make any woman feel sexy, but walking beside a man like my Russian savage is the stuff of dreams, not the nightmare that I expected.

As I eat the meal, my thoughts turn to the life bomb he dropped into the conversation before we left his friend's plane, and I just can't get my head around it. He must be mistaken because I have loving parents. In fact, they must be out of their mind with worry, and it strikes me that I haven't even considered how they must be feeling this whole time. I am so caught up in my own adventure, the enormity of the situation hasn't hit me yet and now as I reflect on it during one of my rare moments alone, I am starting to realize just how much trouble we're in.

Has my father paid the ransom yet? Does he really owe the bratva money, or was it all a lie to conceal the real reason I'm here? I'm the daughter of a mafia boss. This just can't be true and yet if it is, what will that mean for me? The most hated mafia boss in the world, Ivan said. That doesn't sound good and hearing Ivan's tales of his own upbringing, I am starting to panic in a big way. In fact, the food has turned to dust in my mouth as I contemplate being traded and handed over to a desperate criminal.

I will never see my parents again. I will be forced to marry someone old enough to be my father, like Winter was. The fact that Ivan and his friends are going to so much trouble to get her back means her life is shit right now and I'm the unlucky one who will take her place. I don't matter. I'm expendable and they will use me to release her from the madness.

Everything is weighing heavily on my mind and without thinking, I seize the glass of red wine the stewardess provided with my meal and gulp it down as if it's water.

If anything, it makes the whole thing better for a brief period and I rest my head back against the headrest and close my eyes as I struggle to deal with everything I heard. It's only when the stewardess walks past that I open them and say quickly, "Um, I don't suppose I could get a refill."

She smiles. "Of course, madam."

She is back in no time, and I even contemplate asking her to leave the bottle and no sooner has she filled my glass than I drain it quickly away.

Now I'm feeling better about things, and the warm glow turns to a fuzzy sensation of happiness. All around me, people are going on with their day and I should do the same. Push aside my nightmare and enjoy the time I do have and so I fix on my headphones and prepare to watch a movie in the hope it distracts me from my own shit show of a life.

* * *

A GENTLE SHAKE makes me jump and a kind voice says, "Madam, we are about to land. Please fasten your seat belt."

My eyes are heavy as I open them and remember where I am. The flight, of course, Switzerland. It takes me a moment to gather my thoughts, and that's because they are thumping around my head as if they're river dancing.

Why did I drink wine? I'm a lightweight. I don't drink—ever and now I can see why because it obviously doesn't agree with me. I must be allergic to it, and I'll need an epi-pen or something. I must groan or something because the man across the aisle looks over and smiles sympathetically in my direction and I offer him a shaky one back and whisper, "I'm afraid of flying."

He nods as if that's the only reason for my behavior and not the fact I drank too much. A growl behind makes me jump as Ivan says darkly, "No speaking until we get to Malik's house."

Now I'm really pissed off and decide to completely ignore him because how dare he speak to me like that? I can talk if I want to, and I will as it happens. Just to prove that point, I say to the man brightly, "Are you traveling on business?"

I can almost touch the anger vibrating through the seat behind me as the man nods, smiling brightly. "Yes, I have a business deal to close off. What about you?"

"Same."

Praying to the almighty he doesn't ask what business I'm in, God obviously isn't listening because he says with interest, "What business are you in?"

"Oh, um, lingerie." I say the first thing that comes to mind and regret it immediately his eyes spark with interest.

"That sounds way more interesting than computer technology. Do you design your own pieces?"

The suggestive glint in his eye makes my flesh creep because I can already sense he is picturing me wearing them, and I nod. "Um, yes, you know, just like Victoria Secrets. That's us. Minus the Angels, of course. We have our, um, Honeys."

I'm babbling because now I've gone down this road I can't turn back and I hope like hell something happens to shut this conversation down and then the man says, looking quite animated, "Why don't we hook up?"

I stare at him in horror, and he laughs out loud. "I mean, I run an IT company and we service many businesses like yours."

I don't miss the wink he threw me when he said 'service' and now I'm incredibly uncomfortable.

"Oh, well thanks and everything but…"

He doesn't give up and offers me his business card accompanied by a suggestive wink. "Call me and we'll set something up."

My manners make me lift my hand to take it, but before I can, it is rudely snatched away and a very angry voice says ominously, "The lady doesn't need your service."

I watch the blood drain from the man's face as his card is thrust back at him and obviously the expression on Ivan's face is scaring the shit out of him because he stutters, "Of course, forgive me." before turning and looking in the opposite direction.

Once again, a low menacing growl reaches my ears as he repeats his words from earlier. "No talking."

The frustration is tearing me up inside and biting my lip, I stare out of the window and try to calm my beating heart. I don't know what to think, to feel, or to say anymore because nothing about my life is normal right now and yet I can't lie, I am enjoying myself way more than is good for me.

CHAPTER 16

IVAN

Why is this woman so frustrating to me? Disobeying orders and striking up a conversation just to piss me off.

It did. It pissed me off big time and seeing that creep hit on her made me madder than hell. Nobody talks to her. Not ever. Even in her fucking soulless uniform she was a goddess but dressed in that lingerie as she calls it, underneath a dress that is clinging to her curves that makes me jealous of a fucking dress, has me imagining all the kinds of depraved things I want to do to her. I'm obviously not the only one and if I could, I would have shot this bastard at point blank range just for daring to speak to her.

I am officially screwed and losing my mind over a woman, and yet there is no future for us. Not together, anyway, and so I fight back the rage and try to calm the fuck down because the sooner this is over, the better for my sanity.

Only the thought of her anger at the name Malik chose for her makes me relax because I loved seeing the rage in her pretty blue eyes. I almost laughed out loud at the joke, but now the joke's on me because he was sending me a message loud and clear. Stay away from the girl because if I went there, it would start a war.

Sometimes I wonder about Malik. He seems to know everything about us. Our movements, our darkest thoughts and anticipates the problems before they grow. It's why Angelo trusts him so much.

Angelo, otherwise known as The Boss, comes up with the plans and Malik makes them happen. Flynn is our silent weapon, somehow having the ability to get into places none of us could ever imagine and Alessandro and myself are the muscle. The brawn behind the brains and together we make the perfect team. Thinking of my beast of a friend, my heart thumps with pain for him. He has more of an interest in Winter than anyone because I'm not stupid and understand they got a lot closer at Rockwell Academy than any of us thought. He is going through hell, and this will be more difficult for him because Angelo's plan to free his sister requires Alessandro to surrender his soul to the devil, otherwise known as his grandfather.

Alessandro's family history runs deep, and his grandfather commands the biggest mafia operation in Sicily. He wants his grandson to step up and take over from him, but he prefers to make movies in Hollywood and keep his distance from crime. In engaging his families help with getting Winter back, Alessandro must agree to his grandfather's demands, and I know my friend, he will do whatever is necessary to bring her home which is why I must push aside my own desires and do what's right for my friends. All of them.

A dark cloud settles across my heart as the demons claim another soul because Charlotte Richmond is off limits in every way, and I should engage in damage limitation before it's too late.

As the aircraft touches down in Zurich, I set my mood in place knowing the next few days will be the most difficult yet and it has everything to do with the fact I will be locked away in a house with the delectable woman sitting in front of me and if there was ever a test of my resolve, this is it.

As soon as the door opens, we are first off, and I hold her hand tightly to remind her she is my prisoner. Somehow that appears to have been forgotten among all the drama and this is a dangerous situation we are in now.

As we walk quickly along the tunnel, I say harshly, "Remember to play your part. Anybody could be watching us and I'm not talking about the officials."

"What do you mean?" Her voice is a little slurred, which doesn't surprise me given the wine she drank and knowing Charlotte, I'm guessing she's not used to alcohol.

"I mean, even if you think you're safe, it's doubtful you are. You have probably every mafia family in the land looking for you right now."

"Are you kidding me?" She sounds horrified and I snarl. "Open your eyes, Charlotte. You are a mafia princess whether you like it or not, and your dearest daddy is the king. Your best chance of survival right now is holding your hand, so do everything I say and don't question me, got it?"

"Yes." She sounds sulky and I'm guessing, like me, she's bored with this shit already. We are sleep deprived, hungry and running on adrenalin and so the sooner we get to safety, the better for both of us.

I'm surprised when she grips my hand hard and says in a steely voice, "Listen, I'll play by your rules, but on one condition."

"You think you're in a position to start issuing conditions?"

It makes me laugh, and she says angrily, "Yes, I do, you fucking arsehole, because one scream, one word in the right ear and you will be carted off to Alcatraz before you can breathe out."

"Alcatraz isn't a thing anymore. You're so deluded."

"Well, similar then, but I have my demands and you need to meet them."

She sounds absolutely furious, which is the side of her I love the most and so I bite back a grin and say roughly, "And they are...?"

"Answers. I want you to tell me everything, the whole sorry tale, and let me make up my own mind about what I want."

"You have no choice."

We walk quickly but our conversation is loaded with angry whispers, and she bites back, "Maybe not, but you owe it to me to know what's coming. Surely, I should be armed with the information before I'm traded like a fucking mule."

"Watch your fucking language. Ladies don't swear. Didn't they teach you anything at that fancy school of yours?"

"They taught me to fight arseholes like you."

"They did not."

I laugh merely to incense her further and she hisses, "You caught me off-guard. I was in a weak moment. We will revisit it later and I will enjoy wiping that smug bastard grin off your face."

"I'm looking forward to it, princess."

We reach passport control and thank fuck for computers because all we have to do is scan our passports. I'm really hoping that Malik's technology is up to this because one false reading and we could be in trouble. However, knowing my sinister friend, he will have paid off every official in this building already, so I'm kind of relaxed as I pass through the machine.

Luckily, I'm through and look behind and see Charlotte huffing as she tries to get hers to work and rolling my eyes I say tightly, "Other way around. For fuck's sake, you're clueless."

She flashes me an angry look and my cock stirs as it senses an evening of animosity with the delightful creature in my care. I love a good fight; I always have and with a woman like her, the fight is a very different one. Mainly, I'll be fighting my attraction to her because Malik's subliminal message wasn't lost on me. Keep my hands off and I probably know why. If the plan does work and we swap her with Winter, Massimo will be spitting bullets if he ever found out I'd defiled his virgin daughter. It's the mafia way, which is why Angelo was so careful with Winter at Rockwell. If the man she married discovered his wife wasn't a virgin on their wedding night, she wouldn't wake up in the morning. Malik was right to remind me of that and a groan of frustration makes its way out into the world, causing Charlotte to glare at me angrily as she stomps from the passport booth.

"It's not my fault technology is complicated. Actually, mine didn't work, perhaps I should report it. No wonder there are queues at these places."

Grabbing her arm, I say tightly, "The only problem princess, is you, so shut the fuck up and do as you're told before my hand revisits your fucking arse, as you call it."

That does the trick, and she stares at me with pure hatred flashing from her eyes and raises her finger and runs it along her lips, as if zipping it tightly. Despite my frustration, it makes me laugh and the animosity in her expression makes me laugh even harder as I steer her through customs and out through the arrivals hall.

CHAPTER 17

CHARLOTTE

I am tired, grouchy, and completely fed up. Ivan is being impossible and acting as if he's my bodyguard or something. There's also that name I've been saddled with. It's embarrassing and I'm glad I was spared the humiliation of having my passport checked by an actual human and not a machine. In fact, that's probably why the machine failed. It was having its own laugh at my expense. I'm guessing if machines could, it would have transmitted it to all the other machines, and they could have enjoyed a laugh at my expense.

Now I'm delirious because my thoughts are even crazier than me right now and I'm relieved when we head into the arrivals hall and see a man wearing the same uniform as the captain of the private plane, holding up a sign that reads, Mr. and Mrs. Belton.

Ivan chuckles when he sees it and I hiss, "Don't go getting any ideas about the benefits attached to that title."

To my surprise, he grabs my arse hard and whispers, "Trust me, princess, you'll be the one begging for it, not me."

"In your dreams, savage."

I bite back and his low laugh almost makes me smile.

We approach the man, who nods respectfully.

"Sir, madam, please follow me."

I see Ivan dashing out a quick text on his phone, and I'm curious.

"What are you doing?"

He whispers, "Checking this guy is who he says he is."

"Oh."

It strikes me I'm so trusting and luckily for me, Ivan is always one step ahead of the game because I haven't forgotten that we were both poisoned on his own fucking plane. I think he is right to trust no one and against my better judgment, I squeeze his hand a little tighter.

The chauffeur leads us to a large stretch limo outside and I stare in fascination at possibly the ugliest car I have ever seen.

Ivan sighs heavily. "Fucking Malik. Why does he insist on shit like this? We're hardly invisible now."

The chauffeur opens the door and after a quick check inside, Ivan helps me into the sumptuous interior of a car that shouldn't be labeled as such. It's more like a hotel room and as the door closes, I stare around at a form of transport I wasn't expecting.

Ivan leans back in his seat and groans. "Fuck me, I need a drink."

I watch as he presses something and as if by magic, a small bar appears out of nowhere and he seizes the bottle of vodka and flips off the cap, drinking long and deep before gasping with relief.

"Ivan."

I speak his name in my best school mistress' voice.

"Yes, miss."

He grins, flashing his sexy smile that makes me strangely weak at the knees.

"There are labels for men like you and places you can go to for help."

"I doubt that princess."

"That's where you're wrong. My friend Rochelle's father is an alcoholic too and is a member of alcoholic anonymous. Perhaps we should book you in. I mean, the slippery slope and all that, just saying."

I settle back in my seat and cross my legs and don't miss the tortured look he throws me as he runs his gaze down the length of them. Muttering a low 'fuck me', he takes another gulp, making me roll my eyes.

I stare out of the window and sigh. "I don't suppose they have a cup of tea somewhere in this magic cave. I'm gasping."

"I doubt it." Ivan says, sounding exhausted.

"Water then."

"Help yourself. I'm not your servant."

He is irritable and I don't even understand why because if anyone has the right to that title, it's me, so I lean forward and grab a bottle of Evian that is lovely and cold and as I remove the cap, the car swerves and before I register what's happening the cool liquid spurts into his lap, resulting in a steady stream of angry Russian words to pour from his mouth.

As the car turns again, I fall onto him and for a moment, I don't register where I am but soon realize to my horror I am face down on his crotch.

His laughter makes me pull back and, my face burns as I shout, "You told him to do that on purpose."

"Don't be so ridiculous. You see, princess, if you want to suck my dick, it can be arranged."

"I'm a little too late for that because it appears as if you've done the job yourself already from the looks of things."

I smirk when I see the dark stain covering his crotch where the water found its mark and I can't resist laughing hysterically at the fury on his face.

I soon stop laughing though when, without warning, he reaches out and grabs me and I'm hauled across his wet sodden lap and find my dress around my waist. Before I can scream, he runs his hand across my silk covered ass and groans loudly. "Fuck, you were sent to me by Satan himself."

The fact I like his hand on my skin makes me fall silent because this is turning me on to something I wasn't expecting. His touch is gentle as he gently strokes my skin, causing my breath to hitch and my legs to tremble.

Then, without warning, he pulls down my dress and spins me around, so he is holding me like a baby and with a guttural moan, he dips his head and kisses me so hard, I lose my mind. As I reach up, I tangle my fingers in his close-cropped hair and pull him in harder and deeper, so it becomes a frantic clash of tongues, licking, biting and probing, just desperate for a taste.

He pushes me back and his hand runs the length of my legs, reaching underneath the dress and resting on my inner thigh and I am almost panting with lust as I physically ache for him to go further. His fingers hover against the fabric and then push it aside, his thumb caressing my clit, causing me to groan out loud. I am physically panting for him. I will do whatever he asks because I have never experienced anything quite like this and as his finger enters my wet pussy, I bear down on it with all the morals of a prostitute.

He sucks at my neck, and I gasp, arching my back, desperate to be closer than him and suddenly, like the bottle of cold water that fell, he pulls back and says in a ragged breath, "No."

In one swift move he pulls my dress down and pushes me back into my seat, running his fingers through his hair with distraction.

"No." My voice quivers and I feel so rejected as he raises his eyes to mine and says roughly, "I can't, it's not right."

"Fine." I turn away, the tears smarting behind my eyes as I deal with the rejection and I'm surprised when a rough hand finds mine and he says gruffly, "Look at me, princess."

Reluctantly, I do as he says and my heart flutters when I

register the lust burning in his eyes, telling me he feels the same.

"I can't be that man."

"What man?"

"The man who takes a woman with no intention of keeping her."

"But you have, probably a million times already, you told me."

I am so confused and then he stuns me all over again when he says in a broken voice, "But I never wanted to keep any of them."

He drops my hand and reaches for the vodka, and I say nothing. If anything, I know where he's coming from and as soon as he removes the bottle from his lips, I grab it and toss back a mouthful myself. The fiery liquid causes me to cough, which in turn makes him chuckle and just like that, the awkwardness dispels into the atmosphere, leaving me strangely happier than I was a moment ago.

CHAPTER 18

IVAN

*C*harlotte will be my ruin. I already know that because I can't even glance in her direction without wanting a taste. It's consuming me. The insatiable need I have to claim this woman as mine, and that's where the madness sets in because she will *never* be mine.

For the first time, I understand what Alessandro went through with Winter. You can look but not touch, if you want to live, that is. She's so off limits it's not even funny and just that one act of madness has only stoked the fire, not extinguished it.

I lost control and I'm not proud of that.

I understand she is confused. That makes two of us, but I stare moodily out of the window, wondering how we both ended up in this situation. When Angelo told me about my mission, I never gave it a second thought. Kidnap a girl and keep her hidden until we get the call to exchange. I believed this would be easy, which shows me what a fool I am. This is the hardest thing I have ever done in my life and it's because, for the first time, I want something that will never be mine.

"Ivan."

Her soft, hesitant voice reaches me and curls its delicate fingers around my heart, causing me to lash out and say angrily, "I said no talking."

I'm surprised when she edges closer and puts her head on my shoulder, making the bottle freeze in my hands as I raise it to take another sip of something that dulls the pain.

To her credit, she remains silent and as the car takes us ever closer to safety, I wonder if my heart will ever be safe from wanting this woman.

* * *

MALIK'S HOME is as expected. It is dripping in luxury and yet cool and impersonal.

The car stops and the driver opens the door and as we step out into the sunlight, this is a very different scene from the one facing us in Norilsk.

Charlotte grips my hand a little tighter and she may as well be gripping my heart because for some reason I am protective of her. I can see she's scared. Who wouldn't be and yet she only reveals that through little touches and nervous looks when she thinks I'm not looking. She is certainly brave, I'll give her credit for that, which is why I don't shake my hand from hers and merely give it a gentle squeeze of reassurance as we are met at the door by a man who looks as if one puff of air from his lungs would knock us both out.

Dressed all in black with dark shades covering his eyes, he looks of Arabic origin and says in a deep voice, "Mr. Karim told us to expect you. My name is Tariq, and I am your new best friend."

He looks at Charlotte with no expression and I wonder about the secretive world my friend lives in. I know he is in hell with the rest of us and is surrounded by men like this. Strong, for the most part, silent and hiding a thousand secrets behind the blackest shade. He is no different, and a shiver passes through me when I picture the horrors of his world. Mine is what you see. Menace, violence, and unimaginable horrors. Malik's is the same but hidden within the pages of a closed book that you only discover the full horror of when you open it. Torture, emotional mind games and acts of violence, all concealed inside gold lined palaces that appear respectable on the outside but hold the secrets of Hades inside their walls.

We follow Tariq inside and Charlotte gasps at the sight that greets us. It's like walking into a marble-lined cave. The walls appear to be embedded with gold, the hidden lighting making them almost shine, providing light of a very different kind. This is minimalism at its most expensive because the house itself is the art. Rounded pillars lead up to the heavens because we are standing in what appears to be the heart of the home. As I look up, I see a gallery surrounding us and the way up to it is via a huge, winding staircase at the end.

Tariq leads us into a living room that is dominated by two fireplaces, either side of a huge glass wall that looks out on the most breath-taking scenery outside. It's as if we are on top of the world looking down on paradise.

Charlotte whispers, "I'm scared to tread on that rug."

I follow her eyes and agree because on the polished wooden floor lies a cream fur rug that takes up half the room. Low slung cream sofas face the view and that is all the decoration needed in a room that is both elegant, yet cozy and comfortable at the same time.

Tariq hands me an iPad and says in his emotionless voice.

"You access everything from here. Click on the room and a menu will drop down of all the features you can access. If you need food, there is a menu under the food section. If you need to contact me, I am under security. There are four members of staff in the house, all personally chosen by Mr. Karim. You have nothing to fear here. If your safety is compromised, the house goes into lockdown and each room is sealed off. The only way out is through the door marked 'emergency exit' that will unlock when the room is secure. You take the exit, which leads down to a tunnel underneath the house that leads toward the lake where there is a boathouse. Inside is a car, a boat and a motorbike. The keys are in them, and they have full tanks of fuel."

I shake my head because this is impressive and now, I see the extent of my friend's problem. With technology and security like this, he will find it more difficult to escape his hated life and I wonder what his plan is.

Tariq nods respectfully. "I will be monitoring the areas and ask that you remain inside the house for your own safety. As soon as I receive my instructions, I'll be on hand to assist you. In the meantime, relax and make this your home and remember that everything you need is one press of the iPad away. Do you have any questions?"

"Not for now."

To be honest, I just need to sleep this alcohol off, and Charlotte is obviously struck dumb, which is probably a first, so all I want is to be left and hit whatever bed they have made available.

"We just need rest."

I yawn loudly to prove my point, and Tariq nods. "I'll show you to your rooms."

"Room." I stare at him pointedly and Charlotte gasps beside me. Fixing her with a warning glare, we follow Tariq and take the huge staircase up to the second floor. He leads us to another staircase off the galleried landing and we find ourselves in a room that takes my breath away.

Like the living room, this one has an open fireplace on an arched wall, either side of which are floor to ceiling windows looking out across the alps. A strip of lighting runs between the ceiling and the wall and surrounds the room in a warm glow.

The huge bed that dominates the space is placed facing the view and is dripping with silk and cream fur. Charcoal gray and soft taupe cushions designed to break up the palette are scattered in style against the pillows. Huge drapes are secured back from the glass and once again, the furniture is minimal, with no art on the walls. Elegant simplicity is the theme running through this house, and I wish I never had to leave.

Tariq nods with respect and leaves us alone and as soon as the door closes, Charlotte hisses, "Why can't I have my own room?"

As I rip off my jacket, I smirk, "Because in case you have forgotten, you are my prisoner and I need eyes on you at all times."

"Are you sure that's the real reason? I mean, look at this place. It's a fortress."

"With strangers controlling it."

She looks worried and I whisper harshly, "Trust no one, princess, only me, because I am your new best friend. Now I suggest we find the bathroom and wash off this journey and get some sleep because our problems may only just be starting."

I turn away and look down at the iPad to locate the controls for this bedroom and as I enter the huge bathroom, I hate my friend more than I believed possible.

Charlotte's squeal of delight leaves me in no doubt of her own opinion because this isn't a bathroom, it's a fucking spa.

Once again, the main feature is the beautiful view and the ever-present fireplace concealed in the wall. The bath is a huge hot tub that is placed facing the window and the dark marble creates a cozy atmosphere along with the usual concealed LED lighting providing a warm glow.

The shower is set against one wall and resembles a waterfall that you stand in front of and stare out across the view. The toilet is separated by a marble wall and two marble sinks are set in a vanity unit that appears to be edged with gold.

Huge mirrors dominate the room, making it appear as large as a ballroom, not a bathroom, and I am as speechless as Charlotte as I stare around at a place I will never see the like of again.

Charlotte is looking longingly at the hot tub, and I take pity on her and say gruffly, "You can relax. I need to make a few calls, so you have your privacy."

"I do."

Her eyes widen and she looks so happy about that, it makes me feel like a bastard all over again.

"Sure, I'll be next door."

As I leave her to wallow in luxury, I head to the bedroom and close the door, walking over to the window to study the view. As I remove my phone, I hope to God this call tells me what I want to hear because I need to step back onto familiar ground and wrestle my mind and heart away from the delectable prisoner, who is currently starring in every fantasy I ever had as she languishes in the most decadent tub I have ever seen.

"Ivan."

He answers immediately and I say wearily.

"Angelo. I'm just reporting in."

"What happened? You said Norilsk was safe."

"I thought it was. Do you have any information about that?"

"Malik ran a check on the crew of your plane. We guess you must have ingested the poison from something you ate on board."

"What did he find?"

"The flight attendant received a large sum of money into her bank account the day before and after the flight. We did some digging and discovered she has an expensive drug habit and mixes with the wrong company."

"This company, do we know them?"

"Elliott Gardenia."

I expel a breath. Massimo's loyal friend.

"I'm guessing the word is out to all his associates to keep an eye out for his girl."

"Then why poison her? It doesn't make sense."

"You're alive, aren't you?"

Angelo's curt, emotionless voice brings me back to the world we live in, and he growls, *"Think about it. Massimo needed time to react. The best weapon he can wield is to buy him some time. The poison was enough to bring you down until he could collect. Word is, you escaped with moments to spare and your apartment in Norilsk was compromised. They will also have tracked Malik's plane, which was why we arranged the commercial flight under false names. We may have bought you some time, but he will track you down and even Malik's fortress in the mountains won't be enough to stop him from coming."*

"So, the plan is?"

"Sicily."

I spare a thought for my friend Alessandro and say somewhat sadly, "Is the Beast ok with that?"

"He is."

Angelo sounds so emotionless I wonder how he does it because he is anything but when it concerns his sister.

"I'm making the final arrangements and you have a few days at the most. We must wait for Alessandro to clear everything with his grandfather, who will contact Massimo on our behalf. Then we set up the exchange and Winter will be free."

"And Charlotte?"

My heart is heavy when Angelo snaps, *"What about her? She's his problem, not ours."*

Picturing the sweet soft woman currently naked in the room next door, tears my heart out and I snap back, "She is innocent in this. A few days ago, she was living a life faraway from this shit and now she's lost everything. We owe her our protection."

"Ivan."

Angelo's voice is hard and laced with no shit.

"Do your job like we planned. Don't get involved because we are so close to getting Winter back. Do you remember your vow?"

"Don't question my loyalty."

My answer is wrapped in brutality because I would never let my brothers down and being pulled up on it cuts me deep.

A heavy sigh greets me as he lowers his voice.

"I understand this shit is hard. It's why we made the oath to remove our hearts from the situation. Guard yours well, my friend, because emotion has no place in this."

"Emotion is what got us here in the first place." I snap back and he sighs heavily.

"Then we can pick it up and dust it off when the job is done. Your prisoner is not our concern. If anything, she is the most protected one here because Massimo would move heaven and hell to keep her safe and it's up to her to learn how to deal with that. It's not our concern."

"Understood."

His voice softens.

"Get some sleep and enjoy your stay in one of Malik's fuck me homes." He laughs softly. "It's hard to understand why he has a problem with his life when you see how he lives."

"I'm guessing he sees it very differently to us." I remind him that our lives are hidden behind smoke and mirrors, and he sighs heavily.

"You got that right. I'll be in touch and stay strong. We're nearly there."

As he cuts the call, I sink wearily onto the bed and am so conflicted it's like a physical pain. Stay strong, he says. I've always been stronger than most, but for the first time in my life, I feel vulnerable and I'm hating every minute of it.

CHAPTER 19

CHARLOTTE

This is pure heaven. Whoever owns this home is the luckiest man on earth, and that's official. Why does he even leave? It doesn't make sense and I waste no time when Ivan leaves and strip naked in seconds and flick on the hot tub, sinking back against the cushioned sides as the warm water bubbles away my troubles. I only wish Rochelle was here with me. She would love this and as I gaze out over an amazing view, my thoughts return to what I've left behind.

I wonder if the school called the police when they discovered I was gone. Did they imagine I'd run or guess I was taken? It makes me anxious when I think of my mother worrying about my safety. Then there's my father. Does he really owe the Bratva money, or did Ivan just say that to disguise the real reason behind my abduction?

The pain that I've tried so hard to ignore is stabbing me on repeat as I consider what Ivan told me. My father isn't the man I always believed he was. Who is this man everyone fears? The mafia boss we are running from. Just the idea of meeting him makes my soul quiver in fright. This whole situation is so scary I should be crying—permanently. But somehow Ivan has become my only hope. I'm safe with him. He is the only person I trust, which is ironic when he was the man who dropped me into this mess in the first place.

I can't help my attraction to him. When he kissed me in the car, it was as if I had died and gone to heaven. The way my body reacted shocked me a little. It was as if it had a will of its own and I was devastated when he pulled away. It's as if I'm on a quest to discover the woman inside me and shake off the girl who ran from Rose Hall Academy. I am on an adventure of the most dangerous kind—in every way and it's as if I'm floating above the girl I once was and yearning to experience what everyone else takes for granted.

I sigh in delight as the water jets caress my body and ease away the tension. Do people really live this way? I never knew homes like this existed and I wonder how long we will get to enjoy this one. Hopefully longer than the few hours we spent in Russia. I shiver when I remember that place and whoever poisoned us did us a favor because it brought us here.

I hear a movement behind me, and my heart jumps a mile high and as I turn, I look away quickly when an extremely naked savage approaches and I say in a high-pitched voice, "What are you doing?"

"The same as you."

He sounds weary and says roughly, "Room for one more."

To be honest, there's room for ten people in this tub, so I scoot to the other side and shamelessly watch him step inside, my eyes salivating over his body that looks as if it was sculpted by the gods.

A shiver passes through me as I imagine what pleasure I could have with this man and his cocky smirk tells me he knows how to bloody well read minds to add to his talents.

As he sinks back on the cushioned side, he groans. "Fuck me, I need this."

"It is rather splendid, isn't it?" He opens one eye and the

look on his face makes me laugh as he repeats what I said, mimicking my accent. "Splendid."

His low laugh makes me smile and I lie back and close my eyes, murmuring, "Everything we went through was worth this moment. Do people really live like this?"

"It's impressive. I'll give you that."

Opening my eyes, I stare across at him and note the weariness of the man who has done everything to keep us safe and I say softly, "Tell me again why we're here. I have so many questions and, quite frankly, you owe me the answers. It's the least you can do."

A deep sigh is my answer, and he shakes his head. "We'll talk tomorrow."

"But tomorrow may never come."

The sadness in my voice causes him to open his eyes, and he says softly, "Why?"

"Because it hasn't escaped my attention that we are being chased and what if they turn up and override the security system? We could be in danger and, well, I may be sleeping in a different place tomorrow. I need to know the facts, so I'm prepared. You owe me that, at least."

Ivan sits up and the water cascades down his body, causing me to openly stare. He runs his fingers through his hair, looking agitated.

"Fuck, Charlotte, why did you have to bring that shit into the tub? I was trying to take a break from all this."

"Because I deserve answers, you moron." I raise my voice because this man frustrates me in every way possible and I glare at him through flashing eyes, which causes him to stop and stare. For a moment, he looks a little lost and then he says through gritted teeth. "Fine. But not here."

"Why not here? Here is the perfect place."

"Because you're fucking naked, and I can't see past that. Here is not an option because I am trying to cleanse the dirty thoughts running through my head right now and that is never going to happen all the time I am staring temptation in the face and buckling under it."

He glares at me, and I stare back in shock as he reveals that he is feeling the same as me. It's an aching need inside my heart to be close to him. Physically and mentally, and it shocks me because I've never experienced this yearning before. It's as if Ivan is familiar; a homecoming if you like and the thought of walking away from him toward a stranger is an extremely frightening one indeed.

He stands and I gasp as I get the full-frontal view and I almost groan out loud at the rush of need that flows through my body. He obviously isn't feeling it too because he snaps, "Get dressed. We will deal with this shit now, so I can finally get some peace."

As he storms out of the tub, I'm a little nervous now because there is obviously something I'm not going to like heading my way. Briefly, I wonder whether I should be making my own escape plan because suddenly home is looking a lot more attractive to me and now I'm worried that I will never see it again.

CHAPTER 20

IVAN

This woman infuriates me all the time I desire–no crave everything about her. I must be going stir crazy because I don't let women inside my head. I have my fun with them before I leave. There is never a repeat performance, which is why I'm guessing I'm experiencing something different with her. She's off limits and attached firmly to my side, which makes me desire her even more. I'm sure that as soon as she is off my hands, I'll never think of her again.

That's what I keep telling myself and I'll tell her what she wants to learn so badly and then revert back to my role as kidnapper and delivery man because the sooner this is over, the better it will be for my sanity.

Pulling on a robe that hangs in a concealed cupboard set in the wall, I drag one out for Charlotte and try not to stare as I wrap it around her soft, velvet body that I physically ache to taste every inch of.

She looks so adorable as she stands there slightly hesitantly with the gentle flush to her face created by the steam. At least that's what I'm telling myself because I recognize the signs. She's curious and wants to step into the unknown with me.

The trouble is, I'm the same and I'm afraid of the damage that will do to my heart.

So, I pointedly ignore her and head into the bedroom and say roughly, "We'll talk here."

I don't miss the slight tremble to her lip that makes me want to smash something because I put it there. I'm being cold and unfeeling, and it reminds me that she's just a frightened woman alone in the world for the very first time and it's not going to get much better for her.

I sit as far away from her as possible on the edge of the silk-covered bed and note she pulls the fur throw up around her and leans back on the pillows, looking at me from under her insanely long lashes. To be honest, I'm glad of it because having to stare at her curves, that gentle move under the glorious silk of the robe, was blinding me to anything else other than having sex with her.

I get straight to the point and say harshly, "You were born in America, apparently, and your mother died during childbirth."

Her shocked gasp tells me I should have sugar-coated this a little, but it's too late for that, so I brutally carry on. "Your father was away and the people who delivered you were afraid. They guessed he would blame you for her death, and the fact you were a female meant you could be in danger."

I try not to look at her, but catch sight of her reflection in the mirror and the shock on her face doesn't make me feel any better about this.

"You were exchanged with a friend of mine and then you were sent to England to live with a couple known to the woman who delivered you. They died when you were one year old in a car accident."

I risk a glimpse and see an emotionless face staring back at me and I sigh inside, knowing I'm the one responsible.

"Your current family, Lord, and Lady Richmond adopted you and the rest, you know."

For a moment, I let the silence wash away the harsh residue of the reality and then a small voice says, "I'm guessing he found out."

I turn to face her and my heart lurches when I see her lying on her side with her head on the pillow, staring at me through wounded eyes.

"Yes, the child who you were replaced with discovered what happened and confronted him."

"That must have hurt, the child, that is."

It amazes me that she's considering somebody else at all and it twists the emotional knife a little deeper. She is so beautiful at this moment of realization. As if it's not really her I'm talking about. I could be telling her a bedtime story and it impresses me more than anything else. Most girls would be crying and screaming and making it more of a drama than I would like, but not Charlotte Richmond. She is calm, composed and calculating because I can hear her mind spinning from here.

"So, he wants me back, I guess."

Her sad voice hits me hard and I nod. "We are setting up an exchange. Winter will be sent back to us, and you will take her place. Massimo loses a wife but gains a daughter and I'm in no doubt at all he will agree to it."

"Does your friend want to be swapped?"

Her words take me by surprise because I have never questioned how Winter feels about Massimo. I've always believed she is a prisoner of his and desperate to come back to us. However, the stories I've heard to the contrary make me doubt this for a second as I consider what Charlotte said. Flynn told us that Winter appeared to love her husband, despite looking as if her soul had left her years ago. Angelo told the same story and I wonder about their relationship.

It makes me snap. "Of course she wants to leave him. She hates him, and rightly so. Anyone would. The man's a despicable excuse for a human being and I wouldn't wish him on my worst enemy."

As soon as the words leave my lips, I know I've made a huge mistake because Charlotte sits up and draws her knees to her chest and, for the first time since I met her, she breaks down before my eyes. Gentle sobs wreck my heart as she lets everything out, and for the first time in my life, I have no answer. I have no words because I can't deal with this. I'm a fighter, a lover and a savage. Definitely not the person this girl needs in her life and yet I'm all she's got, for now, anyway and I'm the biggest shit of all time knowing I caused her to break.

It's instinctive to reach out and rest my hand on her back in a show of compassion that she shrugs right back in my face with a tearful, "Don't touch me."

I'm so out of my comfort zone I'm falling and yet despite everything, all I want is to comfort her, so with a curse, I pull her back against my chest and hold her shaking body against mine and kiss the top of her head, whispering, "It's ok malyshka, I've got you. Let it all out."

Her tears splash onto my skin that prickles with desire for the tempting beauty in my arms. It's not just because I'm attracted to the packaging, it's the woman inside I crave more than anything right now. My brave, classic English rose that has dealt with this shit in a more impressive way than I would and now I've broken the dam she set in place by heartless words and dismissive comments.

She must feel so alone, so desolate, and as if her world has ended and I am the bastard who made it happen. I have never sank so low in my life and it's not an enjoyable experience.

CHAPTER 21

CHARLOTTE

I can't take anymore. It's too much and as Ivan told me my brutal story, it tore out my heart and left it bleeding into the cracks of insanity. I killed my mother, and my father hates me. He probably wants me back to kill me in revenge. My own parents lied to me all this time by making me believe I was their own flesh and blood. An innocent boy was traded for me and if anyone does, he must understand and then there's the man who is holding me so gently and trying to comfort me who caused my bubble to burst in the first place.

The only person I have now is myself and it's a very lonely place to be. I'm to be traded with someone who has so much love heading her way. She's wanted. I am not. She's the lucky one, I guess, because she gets to start again. I, on the other hand, get to end something I never knew had begun.

Ivan does his best, but I can tell he's uncomfortable and so I drag myself away and say with a deep breath, "It's fine. I'll be ok. The truth sucks and I wish I hadn't asked."

I try to smile and joke through my tears, but the storm in his eyes tells me he's not laughing.

"Charlotte, I…"

I hold up my hand. "It's fine. You did what you had to do and I'm fine with it. This is my life, and I must deal with it. Face my real father and try to work out where I go from there."

"But..."

"No, Ivan. I don't want to hear anymore. Just do what you were instructed to do. I'll be ok."

I swing my legs off the bed and say with a deep breath. "Maybe we should eat and then get some sleep. Everything will seem much better in the morning."

I plaster on a brave face and attempt a smile and then, to my surprise, he follows me and pulls me hard against his body, his arms wrapping around me and holding me so tightly, I don't think I can breathe.

"I will find a way, malyshka."

"What way?" I'm confused, and he sighs heavily and buries his face against my neck and whispers, "I won't send you to him."

It's as if I'm attached to a defibrillator because my heart jumps back to life for a moment and I hate the hope lacing my voice as I whisper, "How?"

He says gruffly. "That's the part I haven't figured out, but I won't give you willingly to him."

"Why not?"

I am so confused and as he pulls back, I gasp at the anger flashing in his eyes mixed with something I can't put a name to.

"Because I don't want to watch you walk away from me, Charlotte. Don't ask me why, but I can't let that happen."

I reach up and hold my hand flat against his cheek and, staring into his eyes, I whisper, "Thank you."

My eyes fill with tears as I grasp the lifeline he's throwing me and as he lowers his lips to mine, I know we are about to step over the line in the sand, and it can't come soon enough for me.

Kissing this savage Russian will never get old. Even during

a complete meltdown, he gives me something pure to cling onto in a life that appears anything but.

With him I feel safe. Don't ask me why, but it's as if I am meant to be with him and I completely understand his comment because if I had to walk away from him, I'm not sure if I could.

I'm guessing it's because he's the only one I can trust right now and the fact everything is different. I'm clinging onto him because I trust him, although the jury is still out on that. Can I trust him? The fact he kidnapped me makes that the craziest thought I've ever had, but there is something between us that is carrying me through the storm. As if he is the lifeboat and I am being taken to safety. With him.

When he pulls back, I almost howl with disappointment and his gruff voice is more comforting than threatening.

"We need to eat. It's been a long day and, like you said, everything will seem better in the morning."

I'm not sure if he even believes that himself, but I sigh and plaster a brave smile on my face.

"Yes, let's see what delights the iPad can offer us."

He nods and walks away to retrieve it and, feeling slightly lost, I sit on the edge of the bed and stare at the dancing flames of the fire. If I had one wish, it would be to freeze this moment because locked in this amazing house, high up in the alps, is like heaven on earth because I am here with him.

The bed dips as he sits beside me, and he holds the iPad between us as we make our section. To be honest, it all looks like the finest cuisine and my mouth is watering at the descriptions alone. We settle on Coq au Vin with a starter of oysters in champagne and Ivan selects a bottle of wine that I wouldn't even know how to pronounce the name of.

As he presses **send**, he looks at me with concern.

"Are you ok, Princess?"

"I think so." I test my heart and find it beating with excitement rather than fear and I say shyly, "Ivan."

"Yes, malyshka."

"Can I ask you a favor?"

"You can try." He laughs softly, and it causes me to smile, and I say with a hint of nerves. "If my life is about to become, well, shall we say, complicated, I was wondering…"

I falter and he nods his encouragement. "Go on."

"Well…" I laugh nervously. "Can we pretend this is an, um, well, date?"

His raised eyes make me say quickly, "It's just that, well, I've never had a proper one and if what you're saying is true, this may be my last chance for one. I know it's not. I mean, well, you would never ask a girl like me out but..."

I'm surprised when a firm hand rests against my mouth and two flashing eyes look at me with amusement and he whispers huskily, "Charlotte Richmond. Would you like to go out to dinner tonight, as my date?"

He grins as he says the word, and I can sense myself blushing as I nod. "I would. Thank you so much for asking."

He laughs and drags his thumb across my lips and whispers, "Then I will pick you up in one hour." He winks and jumps up from the bed and points to the dressing room. "There may be something in there you could use. I'll head next door because according to this iPad, that's Malik's room and, knowing him, there will be a dressing room crammed full of the best outfits that money can buy."

"Then whose room is this?"

I'm interested and he shrugs. "I'm guessing it's a guest room and knowing my friend, he will have provided everything his guests need."

I watch him walk away and as soon as the door closes, it strikes me that this is the first time I've been truly alone in a very long time. At school I'm in a dorm with six other girls and there is never a time one of them isn't nearby. Now I have a room to myself and possibly a treasure trove of delights concealed in the adjoining dressing room, and I can't wait to test out Ivan's theory.

* * *

I WASTE no time and head straight there and it appears he was right because when I pull open the white doors edged in gold, rails of dresses are a feast for my hungry eyes and on further investigation it appears they are not alone. Skirts, tops, jackets and jumpers in every color and fabric make my mouth water and nestling in white velvet lined drawers are silky items of lingerie edged in lace. With a squeal of excitement, I wonder if one hour is long enough and I start pulling out designer dresses and matching underwear as if I'm a kid on Christmas day.

How can one person bounce between heaven and hell without feeling the bruise because one minute I'm in an open pit of despair trying desperately to claw my way out and the next I'm floating on a heavenly cloud without a care in the world? I am currently riding high on one of those clouds and so I suppress any fear left inside me and embrace the moment, because this one could well be the best one of my life.

CHAPTER 22

IVAN

As I expected, Malik's room resembles an exclusive gentleman's outfit store, located at the finest address in the world. I'm guessing he has a carbon copy of this in every house he owns and wonder again about the wealth his family enjoys. A gold lined prison can't be all bad and I just pray his clothes fit me because I'm a little more well defined than my Arab friend.

Settling on a white shirt with black formal trousers, I pull a dinner jacket out and test it for size. It amuses me to be going on a date. I'm not sure I ever have before because I don't date women. I fuck them and send them home. This is as new to me as it is for Charlotte, and I'm surprised to find I'm looking forward to it.

A date sounds just the right thing to put a smile back on both our faces and seeing the pain in her eyes almost made me forget my own mind. If she's hurting, I'm hurting, and I wonder about that. When did she become more to me than a job? I've done shit like this a hundred times before and I'm guessing I will multiple times in my future. But somehow things have changed between us, and it can only be because I've spent longer with her than most. That's all this is, and I must remember that. No emotion, no shit and I must distance myself from her.

But for one night only we can both dream.

Maybe tonight will be a precious memory for both of us to pull out when we need it most because one thing's certain in both our lives, the future is a dark one.

I must be as mad as Massimo telling her I would think of a way to save her. I was caught up in the moment and hated seeing her cry. It wounded my soul and I'm wondering about that. I shouldn't care, but I do, and I'm surprised that this is the hardest thing I have ever done because *she's* involved. A beautiful innocent virgin who has been set free from her cage, only to fall into a steel-clad prison with me and there is no way out of that. She's a mafia princess and I must remember her father is the king. I wouldn't be safe from him if anything ever happened to her, and I must sacrifice her to bring Winter back where she belongs. I keep on telling myself that Charlotte belongs by his side, but it crushes my heart picturing her living in his world of madness.

We have all heard the rumors surrounding Massimo Delauren and none of them are complimentary. A vile bastard of the cruelest kind. A psychotic murderer who kills for pleasure. A man who keeps young men as pets and makes their last days on earth a living hell and I am sending an angel into the fire and will have to stand back and watch her burn.

It's too much to bear and so I sigh heavily and vow to make this night count for both of us. Charlotte wants a dream date. Well, I'll try my best.

* * *

On the hour, I head back to her room and knock gently on the door, and it takes her only a few seconds to open it and I almost step back at the sight dazzling before me.

She looks so beautiful it momentarily stuns me and I openly stare at a transformation so astonishing, I blink to test she is real.

Charlotte is standing tall in ivory satin heels, wearing a dress that looks as if it was crafted by angels. Ivory silk encrusted with small diamonds and lace, with intricate braiding, covers a tightly fitting bodice that causes her breasts to push temptingly against the fabric. Small straps shimmer in the light that rest against her smooth, ivory shoulders. Her arms are bare except for the diamond bracelet that hangs from her wrist and the matching choker momentarily blinds me. She has swept up her long hair on top of her head, causing her slender neck to offer me a bite like the deadliest vampire. The make-up she has used is smoky yet subtle and the slight hint of rouge on her sweet soft lips, is like a beacon to a feral man who has only one thing on his mind. *Her.*

"Do you like it?"

She spins on the spot, giving me a good view, the backless dress hanging low enough to draw my attention to her shapely ass that the fabric is caressing like the most desperate lover. It falls out like a mermaid's tale and spills around her, the silk shimmering slightly as if its gentle waves are lapping against the shore. I'm certain this dress cost thousands of dollars, but the woman wearing it is priceless. I have never seen anyone as beautiful as she is and as she spins back around to face me, my jaw drops and my heart pumps like fury inside me.

This is the moment something happens that takes me by surprise. This is the moment when I discover I have a heart and it's beating so hard for the woman before my eyes. And this is the moment it hits me like a bolt of well-directed lightning. Charlotte Richmond is going nowhere without me by her side.

Now I know how I am going to save her, save us, and I need a moment to think this through.

"You'll do." The dry words make it out and I hate seeing her face fall a little. Now I feel like a bastard because she deserves the fairy tale, but I am no prince. I'm the beast and so I hold out my hand and say slightly on edge, "Shall we?"

Her soft hand finds mine, and she smiles, appearing a little nervous.

"Where are we going?"

She regards me with amusement, and I try so hard to enter into the spirit of the occasion and say playfully, "To the finest restaurant in the world. Nothing is too good for you, princess."

I wink, but it all seems hollow because I can't pretend. I am suddenly afraid for probably the first time in my life. Afraid of losing her, the one woman I can't have because her future is out of my control.

"Is it far?" She keeps up the pretense, and I shake my head. "No, it's closer than you think."

As we walk down the marble hallway toward the dining room, I hope my instructions were carried out. However, as we head inside, I was obviously worrying unnecessarily as Charlotte gasps at the sight before her eyes.

A table has been set by the window where the candlelight of well over one hundred candles, flicker around the room reflected a thousand times over. Two open fires dance on either side of the panoramic window that only serves as a black canvas for the lights to shine against. Candles burn on every surface, including the floor, set in glass lanterns around the perimeter of the room. Huge floral displays create a heady scent, and the polished floor shines as we step across it. The fur rug on the floor has me imagining Charlotte naked on all fours, and I push away the depraved thoughts in my head right now. She deserves better than me and it's up to me to play at being the prince for once because she should have the best on offer and sadly for her, that's me.

I hold out her chair and she glances up at me, her beautiful blue eyes shining with excitement and a blinding smile on her pretty face. "Thank you so much."

She bats her lashes and my heart twists, causing a pain so sharp, it momentarily stops me. I just stare at this natural beauty and experience a craving so strong, I can't deny it, and leaning down, I suck her tempting lower lip into my mouth and can't resist tasting and exploring it deeper. My hand wraps around the back of her head and I pull her in hard and her low moan makes my cock strain against the well-tailored pants I'm wearing. I have never wanted anyone as much as her and I'm struggling with that.

I pull away and say ruefully, "I'm sorry. I couldn't help myself. You look so beautiful." I love how she blushes and sucks in the same bottom lip I feasted on seconds ago and I say almost desperately, "Fuck, I need a drink."

I waste no time and retreat to the other side of the table knowing that I'll need superhuman strength to keep my hands off her and as I sit wondering if I have enough willpower for that, a waiter appears as if in a puff of smoke and says respectfully, "Sir, madam, allow me."

He lifts the champagne I ordered from the ice bucket nearby and pours it into two crystal flutes and leaves as silently as he came. As I lift my glass to hers, I say huskily, "You are the most beautiful woman I have ever seen, and I am the luckiest man alive because you agreed to go out on a date with me."

She touches her glass to mine and says with a soft smile, "Thank you for asking me."

I watch as she takes a sip of the cool liquid and the pleasure in her eyes causes me to smile like a kid who can't believe his luck and she says with a groan, "This is good. You know, I've never been a fan of champagne before, but well this, it's simply exquisite."

Just hearing her clipped British accent makes me hard all over again because she is everything I'm not. Well educated, composed, graceful and poised. Perfect manners and perfect everything and ordinarily would never be seen dead with a brute like me. It's almost painful to look at her knowing it's a fleeting vision in my head and I wonder if I will ever be able to close my eyes again and not see her standing behind them, wearing that dress and playing this evening on repeat in my mind for the rest of my life.

If I knew how to love, I'm guessing this is the closest thing to it and as the waiter arrives with our starter, I settle in for a very difficult evening ahead.

CHAPTER 23

CHARLOTTE

I nearly wet my knickers when I saw Ivan dressed in a dinner suit. I have never desired a man more than I do him, and his rough edges are what I crave the most. The hard gleam in his eye that softens when he doesn't see me looking and slight yearning in his expression when I catch him in an unguarded moment.

When I selected this dress from the others, it was with my savage in mind. I wanted to look my best for him because above everything I need him to want me. Just for one night, so I can experience something I can only get from him, and it's my mission to seduce my captor for purely selfish reasons. I want him to grab my virginity and toss it over the side of the mountain to the ground below in a frantic act of passion that must count for something amazing. Something remarkable because I'm guessing this is my final chance at that, because I know what's coming isn't good. The pity in his eyes and the fact they are so desperate to rescue their friend tells me life with my biological father is going to be anything but cozy.

I try not to think about him, but I'm curious. I suppose it would be strange if I wasn't, so to distract my thoughts away from him, I say shyly, "Tell me about your life in the bratva, Ivan. I want to know everything about you."

I'm surprised when he shakes his head and lifts an oyster across the table toward me. "No. I will not ruin a good evening telling you anything about me because if I did, this wouldn't be the fairy-tale you requested."

"But..." His flashing eyes tell me to stop, and he says gruffly, "Eat."

I open my mouth and as he holds the shell to my lips, he stares into my eyes, making me squirm on my seat, trying not to react to the rush of heat his scorching gaze sends through my body.

The way he is staring causes me to hitch my breath and as I swallow the delicacy, I stare into his eyes the entire time.

What I see reflected in them should scare the pants off me, but it only excites me even more. I know he wants me, and it is most definitely reciprocated and as I let the delicacy slide down my throat, his groan of longing mixed with frustration makes me smile as I raise my own oyster to his lips.

To my surprise, his hand slaps against my own and as he takes down the aphrodisiac, his eyes burn into mine the entire time.

"Ty samaya krasivaya zhenshchina v mire."

"What does that mean?" I stare into his eyes dreamily and he whispers, "You are the most beautiful woman in the world."

I blush and his finger tilts my face to his, and he says firmly, "It's true. You are also the most powerful woman I've ever met because I would do anything for you, and I've never felt like that before."

"Anything?" I smile, but inside my heart is beating frantically, and he nods, his lustful gaze stripping me bare in seconds.

"Anything."

I smile and, pulling back, say sadly, "I wish that was true. I wish things were different and I wish we had a future, Ivan, but I understand that's out of our control."

"We're here now."

I glance up and am surprised to see a softness in his expression I wasn't expecting, and I smile shyly and repeat his words. "We're here now."

"So, malyshka, tell me about your life. What was it like in your school for ladies?"

Laughing, I raise my glass and take another sip and proceed to tell him every gory detail about life in an English finishing school.

As evenings go, this one has been the most pleasurable and the food almost blew my mind. I've never tasted food quite like it and the wine is making my inner glow burn like a raging inferno. Then again, it could be my companion who is responsible for that because he is the hottest man I've ever met. Not that I've met many and as the last crumb is eaten and the bottle emptied, my heart sinks when I sense the magical evening is about to end.

Ivan pushes away his plate and stands, heading to my side and offering me his hand.

"Come."

With a sigh, I take it and he pulls me up so I am facing him and as his hand wraps around my waist, he draws me in close.

Just his hard body against mine makes a shiver of desire fizz through my body and he rests his head against mine and whispers, "I've worked a way out of our situation."

"You have." Hope flares in my heart as his words reignite a flame I guessed was about to extinguish.

I'm shocked when he drops to his knee, still holding my hand, and says with a slight catch to his voice.

"Will you marry me, Charlotte Richmond?"

I'm not sure I heard him right and hesitate for a second and his eyes burn into mine as he regards me with a slightly nervous expression.

"Marry you, but how?"

"I asked you a question, princess."

The command in his voice makes me blink and stare at him in shock and a warm sensation slides through my body, replacing the chill with the most delicious warm glow. Marry him? That never occurred to me at all, but now it has, I am more than happy he asked. Marry my Russian savage. The man who kidnapped me and took me on the adventure of a lifetime. The man who has acted the perfect gentleman and opened my eyes to love. Marry the dark stranger who causes my blood to sizzle and my mind to scramble and now he is offering me a way out of madness because marriage to him may be just my get out of jail free card.

"I'm still waiting." His firm voice reaches me, and I say with tears in my eyes, "I can't ask you to sacrifice yourself for me."

"I'm the one asking, not you."

Watching him on his knees before me tears at my heart and dropping to my knees, I stare him straight in the eye and whisper, "I would like nothing more than to marry you, Ivan. You're everything I never knew I wanted, but now you're here, I never want anyone else. You have crept into my heart and breathed life into it, and now you want to give me my life back at a personal cost to you. How can I say yes, knowing you are only being kind and doing something to get me out of a sticky situation? I care too much to allow you to sacrifice yourself for me, but I love you for asking."

He stares long and hard into my eyes and says with a husky edge to his voice, "I'm not doing this to save you, Charlotte. I'm doing this to save myself."

To my surprise, he presses his lips to mine gently and whispers against them. "I can't let you walk away from me because it would destroy me. Somehow through this madness, I have found someone special and I'm not foolish enough to let them walk away without a fight. Let me save you, Charlotte, and you can save me right back because together we will make the strongest team."

The tears drench my perfectly made-up face as I kiss him back and whisper, "Then yes, I will marry you, Ivan the savage, because I kind of like the idea of saving you right back."

As we kneel on the fur rug surrounded by cheering candlelight, I kiss my prince with all the romance of a fairy-tale. This may not last as long as it takes the candles to burn out, but I'm not turning my back on the only happiness I have ever had in my life. He makes me happy. He completes me and imagining being his wife makes me the proudest woman in the world, because who wouldn't want this man to be their husband? He is everything.

CHAPTER 24

IVAN

Throughout dinner, I thought of little else. The idea came to me like a bolt of lightning when I was getting ready. Marriage between us would whip the rug out from under Massimo's feet. She would belong to me, to the Bratva and there is nothing he could do that wouldn't start a war. It's our way. Family is everything and a mafia wife is protected for as long as she carries that title. Only her husband determines her fate, and like my friends, I will marry for power. Power over my enemy and in doing so, I will set Charlotte free.

I'm not sure if my friends will see it quite as clearly and I'm strangely nervous about that. After all, it may backfire on us spectacularly and Winter may suffer the consequences, but I have to try at least. Charlotte is going nowhere without me by her side.

As I kiss my future bride, I know we need to act fast because time is against us and as much as I want to seal this deal tonight, I kind of want to give Charlotte the complete fairy-tale and our night of passion will be as husband and wife.

As it should be and just as I told her, a mafia bride needs to be a virgin on her wedding night.

That's why this is urgent because I want to be buried deep inside her virgin pussy as soon as possible, because claiming this woman as my wife is everything to me and not just because of sex.

Because of her.

Because she is the one spark of light in my black heart and is melting the ice inside me. I crave her; I desire her, and I want her, and I want to do it in the right way for her.

I pull away and say huskily, "I'll arrange for a priest to visit and make this official. We will be husband and wife as soon as I can arrange it, but it may be a race against time."

The fact she looks so anxious makes me kiss her again, like a dying man enjoying his last wish. Now I've reasoned with my feelings for her, I am more afraid than ever because losing Charlotte would rip out my heart and I may never survive from that and making her my wife will save us both. I wasn't kidding about that and with her beside me, I see a different future than the one I always imagined.

I wonder what's running through her pretty mind. As we walk back to the guest room, I'm guessing she's worried. Hell, I'm worried because I've made a decision that could potentially change everyone's lives and the people it affects may not understand.

Charlotte's voice quivers slightly as she says in a hushed whisper, "Ivan."

"Yes, princess."

"I didn't just dream that. You really did ask me to marry you."

"I did."

"And I really said yes."

"You did."

I chuckle softly as she stops and wraps her arms around my waist and lays her head on my chest and says sweetly, "Thank you for asking."

I roll my eyes. "Forever the finished lady, aren't you, Princess? There's no need to thank me because I should be the one thanking you."

"Why?" She really doesn't get it and I lift her face to mine and say huskily, "Because regardless of our current situation, I would have asked, anyway."

The delight in her eyes makes me so happy and I can't remember ever feeling like this. It's as if a great weight has fallen from my soul and I am free for probably the first time in my life. Being around an innocent lady like Charlotte makes *me* better. I think before I act, and I consider the consequences of all my words and actions on how she will react to them.

As I stroke her face lightly, I love how her eyes close, and she smiles softly and leans into my hand. She is like a delicate butterfly I need to handle with care, and I can't resist leaning down and brushing my lips against her delicate ones before whispering, "Go and get ready for bed. I need to make a call."

She nods and as I open the door for her, I take a moment to watch her glide across the room before disappearing into the dressing room.

Then like a man heading off to face judgment day, I walk back to the living room and dread the next call I must make.

* * *

IT'S as if time freezes as I contemplate my next conversation and, for Dutch courage, I pour myself a glass of whiskey and sit on the couch, staring into the flames flickering in the fireplace and take a deep breath.

Then I make the call that will change everything.

"Ivan."

"Angelo."

"Is everything ok?"

"It couldn't be better. This place is a fucking palace."

His low laugh tells me I've caught him in a good mood, so I don't even hesitate.

"I need a favor."

"Which is?"

"You need to arrange a priest. I'm getting married to Charlotte."

His silence tells me everything, and I steel myself for what's coming, but to my surprise, he just says, *"Congratulations."*

"You're not mad."

I'm astonished and a low laugh echoes in my ear.

"It was always a possibility."

"What does that mean?"

"It means I understand you, Ivan, and you've always been a sucker for a pretty girl. I also know that you've never spent two days in the company with the same one and spending time with a woman who looks like Charlotte was like pouring gasoline on an open fire. You see, Ivan, I kind of get how that can hit you because it happened to me. I'm guessing Flynn can say the same, so yes, it was always a possibility, because we all want the same thing."

"Power."

He laughs out loud. *"I've learned true power comes from the women we fall in love with. I'm guessing you're experiencing that now. You will do anything for her, despite the personal cost, and that is why I know you've fallen hard."*

"But Winter? It could screw things up."

"Only if we reveal all our cards."

For the first time in this conversation, I breathe a sigh of relief and remember who I'm talking to. We call Angelo the boss for a very good reason because he is the brains behind everything we do. He sees things none of us even anticipate coming and has an answer for every eventuality. Knowing him, he will have planned for this and already has a priest on speed dial who can be available at a moment's notice.

"So, as I said, congratulations. You get married in the morning. 9 am. There is no time to hang around."

"Have you heard from Massimo?"

I'm curious about that and Angelo's low laugh makes me smile.

"It was amusing watching him tear down cities for information and call in every favor he's owed. It wasn't long before word got back to him about your trip to Russia and I heard he's spitting fire that you got away. It won't be long before he connects the dots that lead him to you, so the sooner we arrange your flight to Sicily, the better."

"You mean he knows we're here?"

"I'm guessing he will discover that soon enough, so we must always be one step ahead. Alessandro is currently dealing with his grandfather and as soon as we receive orders to show up there, we continue to observe and react to the situation."

"And Don Majerio will agree?"

"I know he will agree. He wants Alessandro by his side and will honor any deal to make that happen. We want Winter and he will make the arrangements to bring her home."

"But Charlotte?"

I falter as I say her name and Angelo says in a softer voice. "Leave it with me, my friend. I'll figure out a way we all get what we want, except Massimo, of course. That will be the sweetest part of the plan. Revenge."

He sighs and says wearily, "I must go. There is a lot to organize. Pass on my commiserations to your bride. I'll send flowers."

His low chuckle is soon cut off as he ends the call, and I'm happier than I felt a few minutes ago. I'm not sure why I ever doubted his own loyalty. We are blood brothers and that counts for a lot. It means everything knowing I have his support and now I must care for a woman I crave more than anything in life. It's up to me to determine our future, and if Massimo thinks he's taking her from me, I'm prepared to do whatever it takes to stop that from happening.

CHAPTER 25

CHARLOTTE

I must be dreaming. I'm engaged to be married to a criminal. A hot, dangerous criminal who makes me shiver with desire whenever I see him. It's not lust sprinting away with my senses, either. I genuinely enjoy his company. He makes me laugh and I'm comfortable around him. I never imagined this would be an option, but now I think of it, it's the perfect one. He will be my husband, and everyone knows a wife belongs by his side. My biological father won't be able to do anything about it and I can breathe easier knowing I have a better future than before.

It turns my thoughts to Winter. The woman responsible for everything, and I wonder where this leaves her. If there is no exchange, how will she be set free? I'm worried about that because it's so important to Ivan. He must have a plan, surely. At least I hope he does because even I can tell this isn't over yet and things may not work out how we want them to.

I change into the sexiest nightie I can find, and love Ivan's friend's taste in clothes. Everything feels so good against my skin and I have more than enough amazing outfits to choose from. I wonder if he's married himself and this is his wife's doing. I hope so, anyway, because right at this moment, I want everyone in the world to be as happy as I am now.

I crawl under the silken sheets and stretch with satisfaction, loving how comfortable this bed is and brimming with anticipation for what happens next. Will it be tonight? Will I finally lose something I am keen to leave in the past? I want to discover what's making my body so interested. To finally understand the secret everyone is intrigued about. To discover what happens when a man loves a woman and I'm in no doubt that I want him. It's up to me to keep him interested because now I've found him, I'm scared of losing him as quickly.

The door opens and my pulse races as I glance up and smile shyly. As always, my heart flutters as soon as I see him, and the heat builds inside as I wait for what happens next.

To my surprise, he sits on the edge of the bed and smiles, and I sense his relief as he exhales. "The priest will be here at 9 am."

"He will?" I stare at him in surprise, and he nods, looking extremely pleased with himself.

"Yes, princess, tomorrow we become husband and wife and I can't wait to show you just how much I want you."

I don't miss his choice of words and am a little disappointed about that. I suppose it's too much to hope for him to love me. Especially after only a few days, but I already believe I love him. If I didn't, why do I feel so empty inside at the idea of leaving him and why does every word from his lips make me smile, even when he's angry? I search for him at all times and my breath hitches when he is close. I want to care for him and make him happy, so if that isn't love, I don't know what is.

Perhaps this is another part of his job, and he is lying to me. I must remember he's a hard criminal who doesn't play by the rules. Does that include love? Is this part of his plan? My heart sinks when he says with a sigh, "I'll sleep in Malik's room tonight. We do this properly."

"But you said you needed to keep me with you because I'm your prisoner. Has that changed?"

I try to make light of it, but I'm panicking right now at the prospect of being apart from him for a second and he smiles softly and lifts my hand, before kissing it sweetly in a lovely act of gallantry.

"I want to do what's right for you, Charlotte. I want our wedding night to be the most special night of our lives. I want to start as I mean to go on and give you the world, and it may not be your dream wedding, but it will be mine."

"Yours. You mean you dreamed of getting married? I find that hard to believe."

I giggle as he groans. "I hadn't met you yet. Of course, I didn't want to get married, but shit happens and then you're fucked."

He winks and I stifle a grin as he stands and throws another tortured gaze my way. "I'll be next door. Try and get some sleep because I promise you one thing, you won't be getting any tomorrow."

He smirks as he turns and walks away, leaving me both elated and frustrated. So near and yet so far and tomorrow can't come soon enough for me.

SOMEHOW, I do manage to get some sleep and as the dawn rises, I wake with hope for the first time in many years. Today I marry the man of my nightmares. Who guessed there would be a fine line between the two?

He is everything I shouldn't want but crave, like a drug. My rough Bratva bastard and yet beneath the rage and tattoos beats a golden heart that I am lucky enough to call mine.

A gentle knock at the door makes me jump and I call out, "It's ok, you can come in."

Expecting Ivan, I'm surprised when a woman enters who smiles and says warmly, "Good morning my dear. I am here to assist you."

"You are?" I'm slightly nervous because what if this is a trap? She could be anyone and yet I find that hard to comprehend because she leaves, and then immediately returns, pushing a trolley laden with breakfast things.

"First, you must eat while I fill you a bath. Mr. Volkov asked me to inform you that it's bad luck to see the bride before the wedding and he is taking this seriously."

It makes me giggle picturing Ivan playing by rules other than his own, and the woman smiles and offers me her hand.

"Allow me to introduce myself. I'm Greta Keller, the housekeeper here. My husband works with me, and we take care of this home for the family, making sure it's always ready for last minute guests."

"You do a good job; it's amazing."

"It is. We are very lucky."

"Do you live here, then?" I'm interested to meet another person at last and it's good to have a conversation without Ivan growling behind me.

She nods. "We have an apartment on the lower level. Most of the time we're alone, but occasionally one of the family heads our way, allowing us to earn our extremely generous wages."

She loads up a tray and brings it over to the bed and it's as if I'm a queen enjoying the perfect breakfast. I see the croissants and pastries nestling in a napkin in a silver bowl and could get used to this. Little silver pots of preserves accompany it, and she asks, "Tea or coffee."

"Oh, tea please. English breakfast if you have it."

"Of course, ma'am. We have everything."

As I glance around me, I really think she does and as I enjoy the light meal, I'm so happy to be here and any nerves I may have had were left behind in the night.

CHAPTER 26

IVAN

I couldn't sleep. Being away from Charlotte for longer than a few minutes makes me anxious. What if something happens to her and I'm not there? So, rather than sleep in Malik's bed, I slept outside her room because fuck if anything is going to happen to her when I'm around. It was pure torture as images of her sleeping in a silk paradise, wearing that sexy nightdress she selected, made me wild and wish tomorrow was here already. I'm impatient to make her mine in every way, and once my ring is on her finger, she will never get away from me.

As I twist my own ring, I already know this is the one I'm marrying her with. It belonged to my grandfather. He was the only man I've ever looked up to because he was wise and never foolish and stayed loyal to my grandmother his entire life. Unlike my own father, who always has a steady stream of women and never marries any of them.

My mother left, apparently, but I don't believe that for a second because it appears he has made it his mission in life to screw as many women as he can. Sometimes even more than one.

I vow to be like my grandfather and will stay loyal to my princess, and as soon as this shit is over, we will go shopping for a ring fit for a queen. Nothing will ever be good enough for her and I will give her the world and God help anyone who tries to step in the way of that. I'm a fighter for a reason and I crave the violence. I love this life because it gives me the adrenalin fix I need to survive. I fight because I love to fight, and I doubt that will ever change. It's ironic that such a gentle beauty has captured my heart with her small smile and touch of innocence because, unlike any woman I've met before, Charlotte blows through my world like a breath of the purest air.

I barely slept all night. The thoughts that ran through my mind were like the most toxic river. Am I being selfish? Interfering in a plan just because I've met one woman who interests me more than most. Is this fair to her, swapping one mad prison for another?

Marriage for power was the plan. My own was intended on being with a mafia princess of a rival family. To cement our union and earn the loyalty of her father so he could offer much needed backup when we wage war on Massimo.

We never thought for a second he had a daughter and especially not to marry into the family of the one man we all seek to destroy. I wonder how Charlotte will feel when we murder her father in cold blood before she even gets to call him daddy?

So many tortured thoughts act like knives to my soul as I lie thinking about what a fool I am. This marriage is only good for one person — me. I want that emotion she drags from inside me when she opens her pretty little mouth and speaks in her posh accent. I crave her youthful innocence, even though she is the same age as me. Unlike me who grew up way too fast, she was locked away in a school for young ladies not knowing anything of the harsh realities of the world and yet I'm the bastard who wants to toss her headfirst into hell and jump in behind her because hell has been my home all my life. It just makes it easier to burn when you have someone to keep you company.

The morning breaks and I can't back down now. My mind was set and nothing I tried shifted it. Charlotte somehow became mine between annoying the hell out of me and becoming my everything. The brave way she endured the horrors that unfolded and never really complained impressed me. She took it all in her stride and maintained her good humor and I love that about her. She is the light to my darkest shade and edges everything in rainbows and pixie dust. She makes everything worthwhile and I haven't even explored the part of her yet that interests me like a physical ache. Her body. I want to crawl inside and hide from the world because Charlotte makes me look at things differently.

So now my biggest test will be keeping her safe and by my side and for a fighter who exists to fight, I'm more than up for the challenge. Unlike Winter, Massimo is not getting his hands on any part of my woman and there will be devastation if he tries.

Tariq joins me in Malik's room and arranges some food. Not that I'm hungry, but he is right to make me try at least.

"Any word on the priest?" I say as I sip my third espresso and he nods. "Ten minutes away."

I nod. "Anything to report?"

He says in his emotionless voice, "There is no intelligence telling me that Massimo knows where you are. We have people monitoring his movements and our spies at the airport are on duty to report back if he arrives. It's the same at the port and the rail station. We have it covered."

"You think you do, but knowing Massimo, he will find a way."

Tariq nods because he can't disagree with that. We both

understand who we are dealing with, and I wouldn't put it past Massimo to disguise himself as the priest and slay me before my own bride.

"The priest." I say gruffly, "Does he check out?"

"Perfectly. He has lived here for thirty years and performed many services at the church. He is known and there is no scandal attached to his name or secrets he is hiding. We will carry out a search when he arrives and only when he's passed that will he be allowed inside the main house."

"And the witnesses?"

"Myself and Mrs. Keller."

I nod. "Good. The sooner we get this done, the happier I'll be."

Tariq nods and leaves me to change and as I pull on the ever-present black suit and white shirt, I fasten the tie and step back, hating the reflection that hurts my eyes. I've always found it hard to look at myself. I'm guessing it's why I've inked so many pictures and words on my skin. I hide behind them because I don't like what I see. A cold-blooded killer who never shows mercy. This is the first time I've felt any emotion at all and that was the deciding factor in my decision. I have a new role now which is to protect my princess because if anyone hurts or upsets her in any way, they will suffer the effects of that because I'm an unforgiving bastard and will take the greatest pleasure in making sure they never do it again.

Ten minutes later and Tariq returns. "It's time."

I follow him toward the door leading outside.

It appears the staff have been busy because they've decorated the gazebo that overlooks the Alps with the most beautiful flowers and drapes of silk tied up with huge trailing satin bows. It looks magical and for the first time, there is a lump in my throat because I want this to be perfect for her. My blushing bride and I am excited to see her when she stands beside me because that's where she belongs, where we both belong, and I already know I will never be happy if she is not there.

CHAPTER 27

CHARLOTTE

I am so excited I almost can't walk. My legs are shaking, and my eyes are watering because I am so emotional. My wedding day. I never expected one quite like this one and as I step back and stare at myself in the mirror, I can't quite believe the woman looking back at me.

Somehow Greta has pulled off a miracle and as fairy godmothers go, she is a talented one because from out of nowhere, she rustled up an exquisite bridal gown that is much better than I would ever choose.

Ivory silk is encrusted with diamonds but unlike my evening dress, this one is absolutely huge. It makes me seem so small inside it and as I stare in awe at the folds of taffeta that flare to the ground and trail behind me; I swallow the lump in my throat as I struggle to breathe. Ivan calls me Princess and I am beginning to believe it myself. The diamonds that sparkle around my neck almost blind me and the intricate way Greta has styled my hair makes my face seem smaller, more delicate even, as it sits in a chignon pulled back from my face. She has woven diamonds into it which scares me to death because despite what she said, I can tell these babies are real ones and not the fake ones she pretended they were.

My make-up is polished perfection and yet looks so natural I wouldn't know it was there and I sat like a statue while Greta went about her work, and she created a masterpiece.

"You are perfect, Charlotte; you are such a beautiful bride." The admiration in her voice makes me happy and it must show in my smile because she laughs. "Oh, to be young and in love."

Her words bounce around me like a delicious dream. Love. Is this what I'm experiencing right now? Ivan isn't the kind of love I thought I'd find. If anything, the complete opposite, and I wonder what my parents would think if they saw me now. It seems so wrong to be making such a monumental life choice without them by my side, but then again, they have their own secrets to hide. The fact they lied to me my entire life isn't sitting well with me at all.

I have a lot to say to them when I'm home, and I trust Ivan to make that happen. I understand we are up against the ticking clock and there is a huge problem looming, but as soon as the dust settles, I want to return to London and make everything right. If they haven't died already from the fact I was kidnapped in the first place, I'm certain they will both have a joint heart attack when they meet their new son-in-law. It makes me smile and Greta grins.

"Well, my darling, it's time to get a husband. Shall we?"

She offers me her arm and I experience a twinge of disappointment inside me, knowing there should be a different person walking by my side. I always imagined my father would be the one to give me away, but it turns out the man who enjoys that title is a stranger to me anyway and hasn't earned the right. So, I smile bravely and follow her outside and it strikes me as we walk, that I never had any doubts I am doing the right thing. I want to marry Ivan and I want to discover what destiny does with us because this could be the start of the most incredible journey of my life.

I am speechless when we round the corner and I see a gazebo resembling a fairy-tale palace set against the most amazing back drop. My eye is drawn immediately to the man standing there, and I swallow any emotion as he watches me approach, intensity standing beside him like a bodyguard. He radiates menace and something else. Desire. It's a powerful thing, being the object of a man's desire and especially a man like him.

With every single step I take, it's like a magnetic pull and I couldn't back out now if I tried. I'm walking headfirst into oblivion and I'm not looking back because I crave this man and everything heading my way and am impatient to become his wife in every sense of the word.

The priest standing by looks at me kindly and as I reach Ivan's side, Greta steps to one side and joins the scary security guard who met us on the first day.

The priest smiles and makes to speak, but before any words make it out of his mouth, Ivan holds up his hand and silences him, making me anxious that something's wrong.

He turns toward me, and I witness pure emotion blazing from Ivan's eyes as he says so softly only I can hear him. "You are beautiful, Charlotte. You are the most perfect princess, but before we go any further, I just want to make sure you are fine with this."

"Ivan." I roll my eyes, which causes him to grin.

"Are you seriously asking me that on my wedding day? Perhaps it is you who is having doubts?"

I cock my head to one side, feeling worried about that, and he takes my hand and says huskily, "I always understood I'd marry. It was going to happen and not because I fell in love. My bride was one of convenience, someone who would give me power to use against my enemies. The mafia way."

I'm not enjoying the turn this conversation is taking, and then he strokes my face and stares deep into my eyes, saying huskily, "Then I met you and I realized what marrying for power really meant. Just imagining a different bride standing beside me caused my heart to physically ache and knowing I must watch you walk away from me was a knife through that heart. When I watched you standing in that beautiful dress last night, it struck me how much you looked like a bride and then it hit me. You were. You were my bride and, as it turns out, the person who has all the power in this marriage is you. That's why I need to know that you want this; you want me because to force you to do something against your wishes means that one day you will walk away from me and that is the only thing in my life so far that has ever truly scared me."

"Fuck, Ivan." I sniff and wipe the tears away from my eyes that are destroying Greta's work of art. He looks concerned as his words hit home and reaching up, I stroke his face and whisper, "I only want you, which is strange but true." I laugh through my tears and fix a frown on my face. "So, nice try savage, but you're not getting off my line so easy. You will marry me and save me from my wicked father, and we will live happily ever after."

Without breaking eye contact for a second, he says firmly,

"We are ready now."

He takes my hands and holds them in his and as we repeat the sacred vows, we both mean every word. Married for power, he says, I kind of understand what he means because being this man's wife means nothing can ever touch me. Nobody can hurt me and life can't knock me down all the time he is by my side.

CHAPTER 28

IVAN

As soon as the priest utters the words, "I now pronounce you husband and wife, you may now kiss your bride." I pull my wife sharply toward me and run my hand around her slender waist. The emotion it creates is different somehow because now I understand what true power is. While holding my wife in my arms, knowing she is meant to be there is a happiness I wasn't expecting and as I wrap my hand around the back of her head and pull her lips to mine, I kiss her with everything I've got. Deep, slow, and torturous as I worship the soft lips that are pressed so firmly against mine. She tastes of mint and salvation and as my tongue swipes around hers, I love how good she makes me feel.

My wife. My woman. Mine.

Now nothing can touch me because all of a sudden my life has purpose, and it begins today. It strikes me that in saving Charlotte, I have saved myself and there is only one thing center stage in my mind right now. Our honeymoon.

Her soft moan into my mouth makes me growl because what happens next has been a long time coming and as our guests melt away, leaving us alone as husband and wife, the only thing I want to do is consummate our marriage.

"Come."

I grab her hand and pull her along with me, and she gasps. "Where are we going?"

"Do you really need to ask?"

"Oh."

Her soft gasp almost makes me groan out loud because just the thought of what comes next makes me impatient to get started. It's not about the sex either, it's her. Just the anticipation of the moment when she truly becomes mine is the sweetest torture. The wedding was merely to make it official in the eyes of the law, but our true marriage is when I look into her eyes embedded deep inside her and know that we are truly husband and wife.

There is no celebration, no congratulations from family and friends, nobody but us, and that makes it even more special somehow.

It won't always be just us. When we leave this place, the future looks uncertain, which is why I'm eager to make the most of this moment with her.

Her dress trails behind her and she almost runs to keep up, and I know she must be worried about what happens next. It's only natural and as we enter Malik's beautiful home, the door closing behind us shuts the whole world out and as we make our way down the marble lined hallway, I swear I can hear her heartbeat bouncing off the smooth, decadent walls.

As soon as we reach the guest bedroom. I stop and experience a physical pain in my heart when I see her pale face reflected in the warm lighting. Despite her nerves, she is looking at me as if she feels the same and I still can't believe I got so lucky.

She swipes her tongue over her bottom lip and bites down

on it with a show of nerves that warns me not to rush this and so I step forward and grin. "Allow me."

Her startled gasp makes me smile as I sweep her up into my arms, kick open the door and carry her over the threshold because despite my upbringing and the fact I never thought I'd want to, I intend on doing everything the right way with Charlotte because she fucking deserves the fairy-tale for as long as I can give it to her.

Her hands lock around my neck and just holding her in my arms causes a wave of protective energy to wrap around me. I love her. I already know that because there is nothing I wouldn't do for the woman who crawled inside my heart and breathed life into one that has lived a hollow life until now.

"Ivan, I'm…"

"Nervous." I drop a light kiss on her lips and whisper, "So am I."

She laughs out loud. "Don't be ridiculous. What have you got to be nervous about?"

As I place her down carefully to the floor, I drag her face to mine and say gruffly, "That I won't be good enough for you."

Her wide eyes fill with tears, and she shakes her head. "You already are."

Her hands rest against my chest and she whispers, "Teach me how to be everything you ever dreamed of."

"You already are."

I echo her words and, reaching behind her, pull down the zip on her dress and ease it gently off her shoulders. As she stands before me dressed in silk temptation, I take a moment to stare at a beauty I never expected to crash into my life. She looks nervous but excited and the blush to her face is something I could stare at all day and as I shrug out of my jacket and remove my shirt and tie, I love watching that expression change into one of lust as she feasts her eyes on my body.

As I unbuckle my belt, I watch her chest rising as she struggles for breath and when I step out of my pants, her eyes shine and her lip trembles as she tries not to look at my hard cock straining toward her.

Pulling her toward me gently, I kiss her long and slow, taking care to keep things at a pace she is happy with and as she moans against my lips, I run my hand across her back and pull the straps down on her lacey bra.

I groan when I feel her breasts pressing against my chest and as she steps out of her panties, I love the fact she's still wearing those killer heels. Naked and tall she stands before me like a goddess and dropping to my knees, I press my face against her pussy, loving her gasp of embarrassment as I take one long delicious lick right up her center. She tastes so sweet, as I always knew she would, and taking her clit into my mouth, I suck gently, loving how good she tastes against my tongue.

The fact she's so wet already gives me the greatest pleasure and her low moans make me so happy I never want this moment to end.

Planting soft kisses all over her body, I work my way up to her breasts and roll each nipple around my tongue in turn. They are so hard, so delicate and yet soft and enticing, and as I reach her lips, I wonder what she thinks when she tastes her arousal that lies on my tongue.

She presses hard against me and whispers, "What do I do now? I want to make it good for you."

"So eager to please, my little princess." I chuckle against her mouth and then, to my surprise, she pulls away and drops to her knees before me, grabbing hold of my cock and tentatively stroking the length of it. "Charlotte you don't…"

"Yes, I do." The gritted determination in her voice tells me she wants the whole of me and I'm certainly not going to argue about that and as she opens her mouth and takes me inside, I groan out loud at the sensation. Her tongue wraps around my cock and she takes me in deep and I move slowly so I don't frighten her. She places her hands on my butt and pulls me in deeper, and I swear I see Nirvana beckoning. Slowly I move in and out and with each exquisite thrust, it's as if an angel is sucking my cock and as it throbs inside her mouth, I can only imagine the delights her pussy is waiting to give me.

It takes all my mental strength not to explode right now and reluctantly I pull out and lift her gently to her feet. "Was that ok?"

The anxiety in her voice causes me to say sternly, "You never need to ask me that. It will always be more than ok because part of me is touching you."

Gently, I take her hand and kiss her fingers one by one and leading her to the bed, I press her down onto the silk sheets and stepping back, I feast my eyes on her naked body, drinking in the sight of perfection and adoring how embarrassed she looks.

"Ivan, I..."

"Hush." I shake my head. "You are perfect, and I want to admire that."

Her heightened color makes me laugh softly and as I join her on the bed, I slowly drag my hand down her soft body and love the softness of her skin. I may have been in a hurry to make her my wife, but I am in no hurry to own her body. I want to take my time and savor every delicious moment of this and despite her embarrassment, I'm going to indulge myself and if it takes all night, I would consider that perfection.

CHAPTER 29

CHARLOTTE

This is the most exquisite torture. Ivan is a warrior, a brutal assassin and a man I never thought would be capable of such gentleness. He looks so fearsome with his tribal inked body and angry flashing eyes as they drag the length of my body, leaving me nowhere to hide.

When I saw him waiting at the edge of the mountain, the sight of him in that suit will live with me my entire life and nothing else mattered but sealing the deal because I wanted him to be my husband so badly it hurt.

Now he is about to claim his prize and I am eager for that. Despite the fact I feel exposed and awkward lying here while he studies my body like a lion standing over its hapless victim, I am desperate for him to strike and put me out of my misery.

I want to know what it's like to be a woman and despite my embarrassment, I love seeing the pure lust in his eyes as he shamelessly stares at every part of me. Just seeing the inked body of the warrior who stole me from life and then promised me a new one makes me impatient to get on with it.

As he joins me and gently presses his lips to every part of me, my body responds to his sweet touches with delight.

It unfolds like a flower against the sun as he licks, sucks and gently nips every inch of skin and the wet trail between my legs tells me I'm more than happy about it.

Once again, he dips his head and I bite back the groan that reminds me what a slut I am for loving every moment of something that should be so wrong. My thighs part to let him in further and I gasp when he sucks on my clit, causing a fresh burst of longing to make me gasp, "That's so good."

His rough hands roam my body and suddenly the urgency increases in the room as he pulls back and growls, "I'm sorry princess, I can't hold back any longer.

"Then don't." A ragged breath accompanies my words and as his hard cock gently teases against my pussy, I am shocked to discover I want him inside me so badly it's become the most important thing in my world.

He grasps my chin and forces me to look into his eyes and the lust in them causes me to groan, then he says fiercely, "This may hurt, but only for a second. Scream, yell, bring the fucking house down and let everyone know you are mine."

I gasp as he pushes in slowly, forcing his way into a place nothing has ever been before and it's so tight, as if he is tearing me apart and I cry out as he destroys my last defense.

"That's it malyshka, scream my name."

"Ivan!" His name rides my agony into the heavens as I experience a sharp pain that has no right being here when I want this so much. The tears pour down my face as I face the fact he's too big for me and I'm not good enough.

It hurts like hell, but I wouldn't change a thing because somehow he is inside me and it's as if I'm possessed. He now owns my mind and body and then strangely, my body starts to adapt to his.

The pain subsides and in its place is a sensation so strong it catches me unaware as he gently moves inside me, his cock searching for the part that gives me the most pleasure. His hard body is rubbing against mine, the glorious friction causing me to arch against him for more.

My fingers tangle in the jagged edges of his hair as he plays with my throbbing clit and as he thrusts again, I groan with knowing that I will never get enough of this. His ragged breathing and low groans of passion excite me and make my pussy drip with even greater need. I am being torn apart by a savage from the inside out and if I was in any doubt about what I'm doing, he pushes every one of them away.

This is where I want to be the most, with him inside me dominating my mind and body and keeping the whole world out. Driving my pleasure and making me complete and as the pressure builds, I scream so hard anyone listening would think he is murdering me, but I can't help it because from out of nowhere a sensation so amazing crashes through my body like a storm in a drought.

The relief is so great it's almost euphoric as my body drags the ultimate pleasure from his. It's like an earthquake shaking every part of me and unsettling it from its foundations. I am shocked when he pulls out and a steady stream of sticky cum spurts against my breasts, dripping down the sides, marking me, owning me and changing my scent forever.

He wasn't kidding. He does own me now and as he leans down and kisses me so hard and deep, it's as if he is entering me from a different place entirely. He has crawled inside my mind, heart and soul and now he's here, I can slam the door and bolt it from the inside. He is home.

My whole body is on fire and as I lie with my head on my husband's chest, I finally know what it's like to feel complete.

I have always known there's something missing. Alone in a crowd, hovering on the edge, watching everyone else appear to have it all worked out. Well, now that person is me because I have worked out I don't want to be anywhere else—ever and it scares me because what if he can't make this threat go away and I am dragged away from him? Even worse, that somehow he doesn't make it and it will all be my fault.

"Does it hurt, malyshka?"

"A little." I wince as it burns and I wonder if this is normal.

"It will be sore for a few days. I'll take it slower next time."

"I liked it." I'm blunt and to the point and his low laughter causes me to smile against his chest.

"You are full of compliments, aren't you, princess?"

"And you love hearing every one of them."

His arm tightens around me, and I feel his heart beating against my cheek as he says gruffly, "You're mine now, and that means forever in my book. There's no getting away from me now."

"Thank fuck for that." I laugh softly. "You had better honor that promise, Savage."

His sudden laugh makes me smile and then, to my surprise, he spins me onto my back and cups my face in his hand. "Thank you."

"What for?"

"For being the woman I am proud to call my wife. For making me believe in miracles and rescuing me from hell."

"I've done nothing."

"Trust me, princess, you have done everything, and I will make it my life's work to keep you safe."

As he kisses me deeply, I pull him even closer because there will never be a minute of every day that I won't want to be in this position. Why would I ever want to be anywhere else than against his impressive body with our souls fused together, shutting out the world?

As the kiss deepens and my body responds to it, I love how his cock presses against me and requests permission to enter for the second time. As he slides in slowly, I enjoy every delicious minute of it and don't even care that I'm painted with his sticky cum. I want the whole of him, whatever that involves because one things certain, I regret nothing and despite the circumstances that brought me here, this is a fairy tale and I'm the princess who found her prince.

CHAPTER 30

IVAN

We wake the next morning and as I openly stare at the sleeping woman beside me I have never been so happy. Her limbs are tangled with mine and her soft breathing causes her to look so perfect in my arms. Charlotte is the most beautiful woman I have ever seen and as she sleeps, her features have relaxed, revealing she deserves that title. I could watch her all day and despite the fact I want to wake her up and carry on where we left off last night, I'm content to watch her and reflect on the best day and night of my life.

We spent the rest of it fucking, cleaning up, eating and fucking again. Greta left food outside the door, and we saw nobody at all. We just stayed in our room and as honeymoons go, this was the perfect one.

There is not any part of her body that hasn't felt my tongue as I made certain to own every inch of her. It became an urgent need to mark every piece of her skin with my scent and brand her as mine. Just experiencing her soft body against mine makes me physically ache for her and I'm not sure what I would do if this plan doesn't work.

Then there are her parents. Lord and Lady Richmond. My

father texted me in the night telling me her father had paid what he owed the Bratva and was expecting her to be returned to him today. There are so many balls in the air, but the only ones causing me concern are my own that are demanding to be buried deep against her throbbing pussy. My head hurts with trying to figure a way out of this mess so I can keep her beside me the entire time.

"Ivan." Her soft husky voice makes me turn my attention to my wife and seeing the perfect beauty in my arms reminds me I'm the luckiest bastard in the world.

"I love you."

Her words hit my heart like an ax splitting a log because I never once imagined that love would ever feature in my life.

She smiles and, opening her amazing blue eyes, she stares at me with so much emotion I forget to breathe.

I reach out and stroke her delicate face and whisper the words I never expected to say. "I love you more."

"No, you don't." She giggles and the light dancing in her eyes makes me smile and I pretend to growl irritably, "Are you arguing with your husband already?"

I can't prevent the shit-eating grin from splitting my face as she nods playfully. "I am."

With a growl, I pounce and trapping her beneath my body, I say roughly, "Perhaps I should dish out the consequences of that. It's obvious you need reminding who's in charge around here."

"Maybe I do." The desire that lights her eyes tells me today could be interesting in more ways than one and as I kick her legs apart, I drive in hard and deep, her agonized scream wrapped in desire.

As I hold her hands above her head, I thrust in hard, loving watching her stretched out under me, groaning as her body takes what it needs from mine. This act of love and domination reminds me of who I really am as I fuck my wife like a savage.

Brutal, hard and extreme, exactly the kind of morning treat I love that causes the heat to flare, the excitement to build, and the day to start off in the perfect way.

As she screams my name when I smash her orgasm from inside her, I pull out and spill my cum, so it drips down her sweat covered body. Despite the fact there were several condoms used last night, this is what I love the most. Painting her body with my own personal blend of paint, marking her as mine and knowing she is loving every second of it.

We clean up and pull on our robes and I fully intend on repeating how we spent yesterday. Here I have no worries and no jobs to do except one. Fuck my wife.

However, fate has another agenda in mind and as we eat breakfast out on the terrace overlooking the mountains, Tariq appears and says abruptly, "Sir, ma'am, I'm sorry to interrupt but I have been informed that Massimo Delauren's jet is heading our way."

Charlotte gasps and I hate seeing the fear in her eyes and I snap, "What's the plan?"

"You leave immediately. I suggest you check your phone."

Tariq reminds me I left my phone behind in the room and with a sigh, I nod. "Fine. We'll be ready inside thirty minutes. What's their eta and how long do we have?"

"Three hours, sir."

I nod and as he leaves us, I say apologetically, "It appears that the honeymoon is over, princess. We are checking out."

"Ivan what if..."

"We will be fine. Trust me."

I stand, cutting the conversation stone dead, and reach for her hand. "We'll talk later. I need to make a call."

As we head back to our room, I curse this life. It has a habit of tearing down any pleasure and replacing it with threats and pain. It makes me even more determined to see this mission through because I am so done with this shit and it's time I stepped up and took control of my life because now it's not just me, I have a family and if I want to increase its numbers, I must make our future a safe one.

* * *

While Charlotte showers and prepares to leave, I grab my phone and see several texts waiting.

The most important one is from the Boss, and it reads,

Club Mafia.

That's all I need to know, and I look at the next one from my father.

Fun's over. Return the girl. Drop her outside the gates of Rose Hall tonight. Use the jet and get your miserable fucking ass back home. I have another job lined up.

Merely seeing a text from him is enough to put me in a foul mood, but imagining his evil eyes sweeping over my bride makes me determined to end the bastard once and for all. I need to think this one through because my father is a powerful man in Russia and his death won't come without consequence.

The first text gives me hope of finding a solution to that, so I send them both the same reply.

Understood.

Sighing, I think of the shit we've got to wallow in before we can breathe a sigh of relief and I head off to find my bride and try not to let my anxiety show.

CHAPTER 31

CHARLOTTE

I'm dressing for an occasion I know nothing about. Above all, I'm sad to leave this bubble we have formed around us. It will always be a happy place for me. Our wedding was like a fairy-tale and the only important people were there. Me and my husband. The brutal savage who plucked me from respectability and led me down a dangerous path. I prayed to live life on the edge but be careful what you wish for because my prayer was granted with bells on.

As we walk behind Tariq, hand in hand down a series of tunnels, my heart beats faster as the sense of danger wraps around me. He explained we can't leave a trail, and the house is currently on lockdown. There will be no way in for Massimo's men, and part of me wonders why we couldn't just hide out here.

Ivan grips my hand a little tighter as we reach a door, and Tariq enters a security code.

As it opens, we step inside a huge warehouse where it appears every kind of vehicle is waiting and tossing Ivan a set of keys, Tariq points to a beat-up SUV and laughs softly.

"Excuse the transport, but it's best not to draw attention to yourselves. You must drive to the border and head for the station and purchase two tickets to Paris where your flight is waiting. We have chartered a private plane to take you to Canada and before you ask, there is no possible way you can be traced, so it should buy you some time."

I stare at him with surprising tears in my eyes because despite his aloof demeanor, Tariq has been our savior.

Ivan slaps him on the back and says roughly, "Thanks, man. I won't forget this."

"I'm just doing my job."

He nods with respect and turns and leaves abruptly, the door closing behind him as he goes and Ivan wastes no time, saying firmly, "Buckle up, princess, our adventure continues."

I watch as he retrieves an envelope from the passenger seat and pulls out passports and a wad of cash that I'm guessing is Euros. As he starts the engine, I'm a little worried because anything could happen now, and I'm not prepared for that.

As he inches forward, I watch the doors to the warehouse open as if by magic and we speed off into the brilliant sunshine surrounded by possibly the best scenery I have ever seen.

Conversation is limited on the drive to the station because I can't shake the dread this journey is causing me. After a while, Ivan says gruffly, "Do you trust me, Charlotte?"

"Of course." I reach out and grasp his hand and as our fingers lace together, he sighs heavily.

"I'm not sure I trust myself right now."

"Why not?"

"Because I'm liable to break a few rules, along with many bones, to keep you with me."

"Is there a chance this won't work out?"

That is the only thing on my mind right now and Ivan says

bitterly, "Over my dead body and I'm sorry to say, when you live my life, that's always a possibility. You should understand what you've taken on. My father is the head of a very powerful Bratva family backed by the Kremlin. They don't play fair, and they break every rule in place to get what they want. The fact I've married you will anger them because now they will have to go back on the deal they made with your father."

"But it's my choice. Let me explain that to him."

"If you get the chance, feel free."

My heart lurches. "Are you saying I may not see my family again?"

That possibility never crossed my mind and despite what I've learned, I can't deal with that and Ivan sighs heavily.

"You must prepare for the worst and hope for the best. If we make it to Canada, we stand a fighting chance."

"Why Canada? What's there?"

"Home."

I stare at him in surprise, and he smiles, despite our situation. "I told you about my brothers from college. Well, the place we are heading for is our command center. We call it Club Mafia. Every single one of us share the same future and past. We are bonded by blood with a vow to change our future. There we work on the plan to free Winter and dispose of our families. Angelo has made that change, as has Flynn. There are three more of us waiting in line, and I'm keen to discover how they can help our situation."

I'm even more nervous now because of how instrumental I am in their plan to free Winter and I'm not sure if his friends will see things in the same way as we do. I wonder if Ivan has really thought this through.

We make it to the station and leaving the car in the car park with the keys under the mat, we head into the huge station to purchase two tickets to Paris.

While we wait, we huddle in the nearby coffee shop and stare into two strong coffees with a feeling of a storm about to break. I am tightly against Ivan's side in the booth, and we are facing the window so he can keep watch for anything suspicious. If anything, I am growing tired of being on the run. Fleeing from what appears to be a fate worse than death, and as I edge a little closer to my husband, I pray for his plan to work.

Trying to lighten the atmosphere, I whisper, "So, I have a husband now and I am keen to see what that involves."

"I thought I demonstrated what that involves, several times, in fact."

His low laugh makes me smile and I say dreamily, "I think it involves a beautiful house facing the sea. I will make it perfect, and you will come home at night to a lovely meal and a wife who missed you."

"Seriously. You really believe that will be our life?"

He laughs out loud, and I say, slightly annoyed. "What's wrong with that?"

"You're no feminist, that's for sure. I thought you'd want to get a job, and I prepared myself for a fight on my hands."

"I can work if I want to. Why would you stop me?"

"And what would you do, princess? I'm guessing you didn't study business in that school of yours."

"I studied shit, Ivan, and you know it." I giggle when I picture the disapproval on my teacher's faces if they saw who I married and I sigh heavily.

"My life was always intended to be one of privilege where the women back up their husbands and attend charity events in their spare time."

"And you wanted that?"

"No, I didn't, but I was given no other option. If I had a choice, I would travel and see the world, perhaps as a stewardess or a holiday rep. I kind of like the idea of that."

"You're traveling now."

"With a maniac chasing me. It's not the kind of holiday they advertise in the brochures, that's for sure."

"You mean vacation." He rolls his eyes and I say imperiously, "I mean holiday. We don't use the term vacation in the English language in reference to travel."

"You are so proper, my princess." He leans forward and whispers, "Then again, I kind of enjoyed shattering that English reserve when I fucked you into oblivion yesterday."

My face flames, causing him to chuckle, and I stiffen when he drops his hand and runs it up my leg underneath my skirt and parts my knickers, running his thumb against my clit. "Always wet for me, malyshka. You are such a dirty girl at heart."

I gasp when his finger plunges deep inside and is soon joined by another. As his thumb caresses my clit, I stiffen and gasp, my eyes rolling in the back of my head as he expertly plays my body like a finely tuned instrument. Whispering into my ear, he says in a steely voice, "Come for me, princess. Show me how much I turn you on."

His finger curls and finds the spot, and he presses his lips against mine swallowing the groan I can't contain as I come all over his fingers. Then I stare in shock as he pulls back and inserts them into my mouth and growls, "Taste how much you love your husband."

As I suck them in, I stare deep into his eyes and am surprised when he pulls away abruptly with a low, "Fuck."

"What?" The haze of lust disappears as quickly as I came and he pulls me up, dragging me after him. "Our train is leaving in two minutes."

As we run through the station, I get a fit of the giggles because this is the craziest thing ever and as we make it with seconds to spare, I try to gain control of my breathing as he pulls me beside him onto a seat in a crowded carriage.

Curious glances are thrown our way because we must appear an odd couple. My drop-dead gorgeous husband, dressed all in black, is glaring aggressively at anyone who even blinks in our direction. I'm guessing the atmosphere in here darkened as soon as we tumbled inside and as we set off, I prepare myself for a difficult journey ahead.

CHAPTER 32

IVAN

I don't like crowds, especially ones where there's no backup, so I spend the entire journey glaring around like a dark, avenging angel. Charlotte rests her head on my shoulder and sleeps for most of the journey, which I'm happy about because it gives me time to think.

Massimo is gaining ground and I may be a fighter, but I'm no match for the mob he always travels with. With the support of my Bratva soldiers and my friend's families, we stand a chance, but not on our own. Just the thought of watching Charlotte disappear into his dark, twisted life fills me with horror and I'm so afraid I'd never see her again. Massimo would have the marriage terminated with the sweep of his signature and a few dark favors and I would probably end up chained to a wall in one of his dungeons while he tortures me mercilessly.

I've overstepped the line and must deal with the consequences of that and so it's imperative we reach Club Mafia and discover where we go from here.

I've never spent such a torturous journey in my life and it's because now I have something to lose. Charlotte. My princess, my wife and the only woman I've ever loved. I know I love her. I wouldn't feel pain like this if I didn't. There's an overwhelming need to keep her beside me, and I hate it when we're apart. I'm guessing it's because of this situation, but then again, I can't imagine a time when this need or this craving will diminish.

* * *

WE REACH Paris and take the journey to the airport, looking over our shoulders the entire time. Knowing Massimo, he will have prepared for this and has more than likely got every airport in Europe covered. However, fate is on our side for once and we reach the desk of the private jet that is scheduled to take us to safety with no problem at all and we are whisked through security and are soon safely onboard the small plane.

Charlotte appears almost disappointed as she looks around. "It's not a patch on your friend's plane."

The rather practical jet looks an ocean apart from the decadent one my friend enjoys, and I shrug. "It's a private company who uses it as a business. It's more practical than luxurious."

She nods as the flight attendant smiles her welcome. "Good afternoon, Mr. and Mrs. Belton."

Charlotte sighs, which makes me smile because I forgot about her hated name. However, she recovers fast and throws the woman a blinding smile. "Thank you. It's a pleasure to meet you."

Biting back my grin, I love how proper my English rose always is. I could watch and listen to her all day in company because she is world's away from my usual companions. Rough soldiers, bastards and prostitutes. Not the prim and proper upper-class daughter of a lord. How the fuck did I get so lucky?

We are shown to two seats that offer spacious travel, although nowhere near as fine as before, and as we sit side by side, I take Charlotte's hand in mine and lace our fingers together.

She leans across and whispers, "How long until we're there?"

"Around eight hours."

"Do you think there's a bedroom on board?"

Her husky whisper causes my cock to wake up and I say with a sigh, "This is as good as it gets, malyshka. The best on offer is to grab a blanket and recline your seat. What can I say? My friend likes to watch his money."

I laugh to myself because Angelo isn't the kind of guy to care how much anything cost but I know he's done this to keep us safe. Massimo wouldn't think twice about a Mr. and Mrs. Belton traveling on business to Canada. I doubt he even knows of Club Mafia because if he does, he would have paid us a visit months ago.

"Tell me about your home."

Charlotte must be a mind reader and I grip her hand a little tighter. "Angelo discovered it soon after we left college. He was looking for a place we could all meet and found a remote piece of land in Canada that can only be reached by air. Roads surround it, but there's a trek across hostile land to reach it and we would spot anyone approaching for miles.

"It sounds like a fortress." Charlotte's eyes are wide, and I nod. "It is. When Angelo's father died, he instructed a house to be built. It happened quickly despite the restrictions in access. The materials were shipped and then transported by land, and it took six months to complete. Like Malik's home, this one has impressive defenses and when we take up residence, we bring our most trusted soldiers with us to provide security."

"Can you trust them? What if they tell Massimo about it? It sounds as if he's a man with many eyes and ears on the ground."

Thinking about the man himself, I hiss, "One thing you

should know about your bastard father is he commands through fear. He is the most hated and depraved mafia boss in the world and his soldiers stay loyal out of fear of what he will do to them if they betray him."

"Surely they could join together if they hate him so much and get rid of him."

Charlotte shrugs as if we're all fucking idiots and just imagining what goes on in his world makes me shiver.

"They wouldn't dare, princess, because Massimo has a way of making shit real. His men are so terrified they fear standing up against him because it's doubtful they would get any backup. Massimo searches out their weakness and exploits that."

"Like what?"

"Their family, kids, even their pets. He does his research and if they displease him, their families suffer the consequences of that. He loves to torture, rape and murder, preferably with an audience and the stories that are whispered in darkened corners about what goes on inside his world, would make Satan himself close the doors of hell and take cover."

Charlotte turns as white as snow and says in a broken voice, "I've heard enough."

She wipes a tear from her eye, and I swear it cuts my heart out.

"Why the tears?"

She shakes her head and says sadly, "Because you were going to send me there. Because your friend is already there and because I'm related to him by blood. What if I'm the same as him? It could be deep inside me and ready to unleash on the world when I least expect it."

Witnessing her genuine concern makes me laugh out loud, and she says angrily, "I don't see what's so funny about this."

"You are."

"Why?"

I twist her face closer to mine and whisper, "Because somehow Massimo produced an angel. I'm guessing this was God's revenge and his antidote to evil. You are *nothing* like him and probably everything your mother was."

"My mother." Charlotte blinks back the tears as she contemplates another person involved in this that she kind of forgot to think about.

"Men like Massimo, like me and my friends, have drowned in the same darkness our entire lives. It's hard, rough and cruel but you kind of get used to it. When you meet somebody good and kind with the beauty of an angel, it draws you in. You want to reach out and touch it. To see what it's like to hold something pure for once in your life. It acts like antiseptic on a deep wound and washes the pain away. You are nothing like him, princess, and never will be, but you are *everything* to me."

As I kiss her trembling lips and feel her tears against my skin, I meant every word I said because Charlotte is my pain relief. She is my angel, and I will not sacrifice her because I would rather die than send her to a man like Massimo Delauren, and I would never be happy again if she wasn't by my side.

As Charlotte wraps her arms around me and kisses me back with a fierceness that gives me so much power, I make a vow to end her miserable father's life by whatever means necessary.

CHAPTER 33

CHARLOTTE

Throughout the flight, I thought about my past. The parents I always understood were my real ones and the ones that, as it turns out, are. It's obvious my biological father is mad. A despicable excuse for a human being and definitely somebody I never want to meet. But my biological mother is the one I'm more curious about. Am I like her as Ivan said? She died in childbirth, apparently, leaving my father devastated. Is that what sent him mad? Mad with grief is a term I've heard before. Is that why he appears to have jumped headfirst into insanity, because of me? Because I killed the love of his life.

Is he searching for me to make me pay for my crime in being born? Will I be his next victim as he takes revenge against the person who took her from him?

I can't even sleep and as Ivan sleeps soundly beside me, this time it's me who keeps watch. I love just staring at him when he doesn't know it and appreciating his raw beauty that I still can't get my fill of. The broad shoulders and muscular body of a fighter is a powerful weapon to use on a woman like me. Knowing what lies underneath the black uniform he always wears causes the heat to set me on fire and the only thing to douse the flames is him inside me.

I picture my own parents. Lord and Lady Richmond, who it appears, have been lying to me my entire life. Did they do it to protect me? I hope so, anyway, because despite everything I love my parents. They have never given me a reason not to and they only want the best for me. They must be worried sick, and I have been so busy having the adventure of a lifetime to spare any thought of what they must be going through right now.

The flight passes the same as any commercial one. Ivan sleeps and only wakes to eat the food the smiling attendant serves us. She doesn't appear to think there's anything strange about us. I'm guessing she has seen many things on this executive jet she lives in most of the time.

We eat the finest food and drink champagne, and it's a world away from where we started this journey. I never want to see Norlisk again, but even that holds a special place in my heart. It's where I first went with Ivan. He thought it was safe, and he was prepared to hide out there with me; keeping me away from what appears to be everyone's worst nightmare, even at a potential personal cost to him.

There are so many questions I need answers for and so much fear, but as long as my husband is by my side, I can deal with everything that life throws at me save for one thing. Losing him.

EIGHT HOURS LATER, we land in Canada and after thanking the crew, we head through passport control and take a cab a short distance away.

Ivan is retreating into himself, and I wonder about that. Is there something I should be worried about coming here? Is he nervous for me?

I'm surprised when we walk out to a gleaming helicopter waiting like a magnificent bird to take us on the short journey to Club Mafia and I sense the excitement stirring inside me again.

"Wow, I've never been in a helicopter before." I gasp and Ivan says with a soft laugh, "Then prepare to fall in love."

He winks as he helps me inside and I can't contain my excitement as the pilot smiles and hands me some headphones.

"Wear these. It will make it more enjoyable."

As Ivan places his own on his head, I do the same and grip his hand tightly as the bird lifts into the air. It's the most amazing sensation and as we leave the ground behind, the buildings look like dots as the helicopter banks to the side, causing me to squeal with delight.

Ivan laughs with me as we experience the most amazing flight over huge rivers and lakes and enjoy the most stunning scenery that even tops the mountain in Switzerland.

He points to various things of interest and as trips go, this is officially the best one of my life. There isn't much between us and the open sky and the way the helicopter flies is as close as to real flying you can get, and I adore the sense of danger that comes as standard.

The pilot puts on a show as he flies through a canyon, making me squeal and close my eyes as the ground races toward us, and at the last minute he pulls up when I think we're going to crash. I laugh in delight when he dips from side to side and it's a rush of adrenalin I could use every day of my life.

"Can we get one?" I shout to Ivan, and he rolls his eyes.

"Anything for you, princess."

His soft smile makes my heart thump with happiness, and I grip his hand and raise it to my lips, kissing him over and over again.

Then he pulls me closer and kisses me in a completely

different way, leaving me in no doubt that he's feeling the same. If I stopped to consider the madness he has brought to my life, I wouldn't believe a word of it, and yet somehow this seems normal to us. As if we are destined to live this way, and I only wish the girls from Rose Hall Academy could see me now.

As we circle in preparation for landing, I stare down in disbelief at a place that is way bigger than I imagined. A sprawling estate of glass and marble, with a huge ornamental lake and an Olympic sized swimming pool, appear completely out of place in the vast land that surrounds it. It's an oasis in the desert, a mirage even, and sparkles like the finest jewel as the sun rays find their mark.

I stare in awe and Ivan says above the noise of the engine, "Welcome home, princess. There is absolutely nothing to fear here."

I nod, wondering if that is true for me because I'm guessing his friends won't be so happy to see me. They need me for a very different reason than Ivan and now he's here among them he may have second thoughts. I spare a thought for the woman driving it all and picturing her with Massimo makes my souls shiver. Does he treat her well? Does she see a different side of him? I certainly hope so because if she is suffering, I couldn't live with myself.

We exit the helicopter into a waiting black SUV and my heart thumps as we are escorted by two men dressed in black, hiding behind their dark sunglasses. They nod to us with respect but there is something incredibly sinister about them, probably because of their frozen expressions that are telling me I'm not out of danger yet.

We sit in the back as we drive the short distance, and I can tell Ivan is deep in concentration from the distracted way he plays with my fingers. It's settled around him like a dense fog and the power is swirling around him like the most brutal armor and it strikes me that he has landed here as a Bratva soldier rather than the husband I love.

We drive through the permitter gates, where men stationed at the entrance are observing our arrival. My heart trembles as I note the guns slung casually across them as they study us, and the realization sets in of what I've signed up for. Mafia isn't just a word, it's a way of life. It comes with danger and desperation and a life nobody would choose willingly. I kind of understand Ivan and his friend's need to control some part of it and I wonder if they can really force change and find happiness here.

We head inside and are met by a man who is older and seems even more unfriendly than the guards who met us.

"Roberto." Ivan nods with respect and Roberto says in a deep voice, "Don Sontauro is waiting."

Ivan nods and takes me by the hand and as we follow the grim-faced guide, I wonder what fate has in store for me now.

CHAPTER 34

IVAN

It's good to be home. This is probably the only place I can truly relax, knowing we are safe from everyone. Experiencing flying with Charlotte was different for me. I've ridden in a helicopter hundreds of times, but none were as enjoyable as that journey. The delight and laughter on her face was infectious, and I was like a kid let loose on Christmas day. I want her to be happy, to smile and to laugh. It makes me happy seeing the pleasure I can give her. Now I'm not so sure it was a good idea bringing her here because I may not like the plan Angelo has in place because this could divide my loyalties and the last thing I want to do is choose between my best friends and the woman I love.

I already know it would be Charlotte, but the last thing I want to do is lose my friends. They are more like brothers to me, anyway, and I may soon be faced with the most impossible decision of my life.

We head inside and hear Roberto announcing our arrival, and Charlotte grips my hand a little tighter for reassurance. I wish I could tell her everything will be fine, but I'm not so sure of that.

"Ivan."

Angelo nods as we enter, standing in his usual spot beside the huge fireplace, a whiskey in hand.

He smiles at Charlotte and says pleasantly, "We meet at last, Miss. Richmond. May I offer you my deepest regrets about your situation."

"I don't understand." Charlotte says nervously, and he grins, "Your marriage to the Savage, of course. As if things weren't bad enough, you got saddled with him."

I roll my eyes as Charlotte giggles, and I can tell she has relaxed a little.

Angelo holds out a glass of whiskey to me and says courteously, "May I fetch you a drink, Miss. Richmond? What is your preference?"

"Oh, well, a white wine would be lovely. Thank you so much."

I share a look with Angelo, and he struggles to keep the huge grin off his face because meeting a lady like Charlotte is unusual in our lives and knowing she is my wife must be the funniest thing he's ever seen.

As he pours her a glass, she says politely, "You have a lovely home, sir."

"Call me Angelo and it's not just my home, it's partly your husband's too, which now makes it yours."

He hands her the glass, and she smiles, "Thank you."

Before I can ask about the plan, the door opens and Roberto says pompously, "Don Vasquez."

As Flynn enters the room, I wonder what he will make of Charlotte. After all, he was made to pay for her sins in Massimo's eyes and he might be resentful of that.

I wrap my hand around her waist and say quickly, "Flynn, meet Charlotte, my wife."

To his credit, Flynn merely smiles and, heading toward us, says in his husky voice, "I heard there was someone madder than me. I'm sorry for your burden, Charlotte."

To Charlotte's surprise, he ditches the formalities and pulls her in for a hug and whispers something in her ear that causes her to giggle.

"Don't listen to him. He's the mad one." I growl but Flynn just shrugs and drops her a wink and gratefully receives his usual glass of whiskey.

He turns and looks at Charlotte and shakes his head. "I can see why we have a problem."

Angelo nods. "Indeed."

"What are we going to do about it?" I must know, and Angelo smiles in his mysterious way. "Malik has the details. He won't be long?"

"And Alessandro?" Of all my friends, he is the one I'm most nervous about. He is my closest brother and yet I'm putting my own needs above his and Winter's.

"He won't be coming." Angelo shrugs.

"Why not?" Now I'm worried and Angelo says with a sigh. "He is currently in Sicily, unpacking."

"You mean ..."

Flynn groans. "Fuck! The poor bastard."

"Flynn, have you forgotten there is a lady in our presence?" Angelo scolds him but it's with a twinkle in his eye and Charlotte says quickly, "The fuck if I care."

It makes my friends laugh out loud, and I roll my eyes and grin. "You must excuse my wife. I removed her from school before she graduated."

Flynn smirks. "More like your heathen ways rubbed off on her. The poor girl. Hasn't she been through enough already?"

Roberto appears again with a curt, "Mr. Karim."

My heart lifts when Malik enters looking like the rich arrogant bastard he is and Charlotte whispers, "Is he the owner of the home and the jet?"

"Yes."

To my surprise, she breaks away and before Malik reaches us, she offers him her hand and says emotionally, "Thank you so much. For rescuing us, giving us a place to stay and making the happiest day of my life perfect."

Malik stops and stares and his usual guarded expression softens a little as he takes Charlotte's hand, and they shake on it. Then I'm in shock as she pulls him in for a hug and whispers something that makes him laugh out loud."

Pulling back, he shakes his head and says, "I had to try at least."

Then he accepts the glass of whiskey from Angelo's hand and knocks it back with one huge gulp.

I whisper, "What did you say to him?"

Charlotte giggles. "I told him his name choice was shit and it had the opposite effect."

Before I can even react, Angelo says briskly, "Now we're all here, I must bring you up to date."

He smiles at Charlotte. "Roberto will show you to your room, but I'm guessing you're anxious about what happens next, so I want to reassure you."

She grips my hand a little tighter as Angelo says darkly. "The plan remains. We have secured the support of Don Majerio and his soldiers. Obviously, Flynn controls his own and, along with mine, we have a small army at our disposal. Pedro Carlos has also assured us of his backing, and we have the use of my wife's family that joined mine when her parents died."

"What do you mean, the plan remains?" I glare around the room with murder in my eyes and Malik snaps, "Relax, Ivan. The plan remains but has altered a little. As soon as Alessandro has arranged everything in Sicily, we position our troops to cause maximum devastation. The exchange will be arranged and when Massimo brings Winter to the agreed handover point, we will all be standing by to make sure he never leaves."

"And you think he will willingly walk into a trap?"

I'm not sure about that, and Malik nods. "He will do anything to get his daughter back. If we keep it neutral and act as if we are keen to help him reunite with his blood, we will convince him that all we want is Winter back with hers. Massimo isn't a fool; he will understand the best thing for everyone is to make the exchange and then everyone is happy."

"Not everyone." I growl and Angelo interrupts. "The exchange *will* happen, but Charlotte won't be going anywhere. You have my word on that."

"It's too risky. I won't agree." I'm so desperate because I don't trust Massimo Delauren an inch and then a sweet voice rings out and says loudly, "For goodness' sake, Ivan, of course I will play my part. We must bring Winter back to us, and if this is the only way that can happen, I will meet with this man. I owe you all so much and I won't let you down. 'He who dares wins,' as they say in England, and I wouldn't be a true brit if I didn't fight the battle to win the war."

My friends stare at her in utter amazement, and it makes me so proud to see her standing defiantly beside me and doing what's right. I couldn't love her more and seizing her hand I drag her close to my side and whisper, "You don't have to do this, princess. We'll bring Winter back another way. We have the soldiers; it will be fine."

She surprises me by pressing her hand flat against my face while looking in my eyes as she whispers, "I love you, Ivan, but if I am to survive this life, I must be part of it. You are all mafia, I am not. How will I know what that involves if I don't dance near the flames? I will have the best protection there is, and I won't be alone. You will be beside me and I kind of rate our chances more than a dusty old has been who needs flinging out with the rubbish. You say he's my father, I disagree. I don't know this man and my own father is probably wondering where I am, so the sooner we deal with this, the sooner I can go and visit him."

Angelo interrupts. "That brings us to my next point. Charlotte needs to phone home and reassure her parents that she's fine and happy. Tell them you're married and convince them you're ok. They are losing their minds and are liable to make this a diplomatic incident if we don't move fast and the last thing we need is the authorities getting involved."

He reaches into his pocket and hands her a phone and says with a smile. "Roberto will show you to your room. Make the call and get some rest. I'm guessing our stay here won't be a long one."

As Roberto opens the door, Charlotte presses her lips to mine and whispers, "Relax. I can fight, remember."

She grins as I growl, "That's what I'm afraid of."

As I watch her walk away, she takes my heart with her because if anything happens to that girl, I will start World War three.

CHAPTER 35

CHARLOTTE

*I*van's room is absolutely huge. Like him, it's dark and brutal, from the charcoal walls to the matching accessories. Black silk sheets dress the biggest emperor sized bed and the charcoal fur throw tops it in decadence. The subdued lighting makes it more mysterious somehow and the chrome tables that hold the largest lamps I have ever seen add a touch of design to an otherwise sterile space.

Roberto leaves me to my own devices, and I walk around exploring a space that stuns me a little. It's a far cry from my parents' home in the Cotswolds. A huge sprawling manor house set amid landscaped gardens with a nearby orchard and kitchen garden. It boasts an ornamental formal garden that encompasses a huge lawn where we play croquet most summers.

Inside we have antique furniture that has been passed down through the years and paintings of the family set against wallpaper that should have been replaced years ago. This is so completely different from that. Poles apart even and I have discovered a new love of modern living that excites me in a way I wasn't expecting.

As I sit on the bed, I spin the phone in my hand and wonder what I'll say to my parents. It's going to be a shock; whatever I tell them, and I take a moment to consider my words.

I take a deep breath and press in the familiar number and my heart beats so fast I wonder if it will put me out of my misery and save me the trouble.

"Lady Richmond."

"Mummy, it's Charlotte."

"Charlotte, oh my God, are you ok? Where are you? I'll come and get you immediately."

"I'm well, I'm, oh, I don't know how to say this. It's a little surprising, but well…"

"Spit it out, Charlotte. What's happened? Do you want me to call the police, phone your father at the House of Lords, what …?"

"It's, well, I'm actually on my honeymoon."

The silence says everything, and I briefly wonder if I've killed my mother; perhaps she had a heart attack and is currently on her way to heaven. Could this be mother number two who has died because of me, a macabre thought, but you have no control of them in a situation like this.

"What did you say?"

The shock is evident in her voice, and I say brightly, "My honeymoon. You see, mummy, I met a wonderful man called Ivan. He's, well, a little different but you'll soon love him as much as I do and well, we're really happy and gosh, I'm babbling on like an idiot but what I wanted to say was, don't worry about me. I'm absolutely fine and will bring him home just as soon as I can."

My heart is beating so loudly I'm sure she must hear it and then she says slowly, *"Ok darling, that's well, super. Anyway, I think it's best if you cut short your honeymoon and bring him home to introduce him to your father. You're not in trouble, we just want to make sure you're ok. Can you do that for me, sweetheart? Please."*

I can tell she's humoring me and she's speaking in that

voice that tells me anything just to get me home. I already know she will do everything in her power to break us up and I inject a touch of steel in my voice as I say sharply, "I told you, mummy, I'm on my honeymoon and happy. So, don't worry about me and I'll be home before you know it. Anyway, pass the message on to daddy and I'll be in touch shortly. Love you, bye."

I quickly end the call because that was a difficult conversation in more ways than one. When I heard her familiar voice it drenched me in homesickness, and I wasn't aware how much I've been putting on a brave face. Suddenly, I'm that little girl again and want my mummy and as I curl up on the huge bed and draw my legs to my chest, I'm more vulnerable than at any time throughout this whole adventure.

I can sense the walls closing in on me, and I wonder what Ivan and his friends are talking about. They needed me to leave the room to discuss the details, and it crosses my mind they could be just humoring me. Maybe I still am the sacrificial lamb and will shortly have a different home to get acquainted with. My life is spinning around me like a ball in a roulette wheel and I can't tell where it will land.

When I met Ivan's friends, I struggled to breathe. Angelo resembled the lord of darkness and as each one entered the room, I felt like Harry Potter surrounded by Death Eaters. They were friendly enough, but the undercurrent of darkness surrounded them, and I saw what I had signed up for. Ivan is no different. I am blind to his faults because in my eyes he can do no wrong, but I already know their world is a place I don't fit in. Yet anyway.

Ever since I met my savage, I have been filled with anticipation, excitement, and adventure. He has taken my world and shaken it upside down and I like the view. If we are to survive, I must play my part and when I stepped up and pledged my soul to them, it wasn't done on a whim. I want to help. I want to repay them all for giving me a shot at a future completely different to the one expected of me.

But will I be good enough? Surely, it's not dangerous for me. The biggest threat is meeting my father but I'm married now and he must respect that, surely.

A thousand dark and broken thoughts litter my mind as I lie in the subdued darkness and it's only when the door opens and lets a little light in that I relax a little.

"Hey." I sit up and stare at my husband and, as always, my heart skips a beat. He looks weary, but there is something about him that's different.

I can't place it and as he sits on the bed, he reaches for me and pulls me tightly against him, his arms wrapping around me and holding me close.

He kisses my head, and don't ask me why, but it feels a lot like goodbye and now I'm afraid, really afraid because what the hell happened in that room when I left?

I whisper against his chest, "What's happening?"

I'm almost afraid of his answer and he says with a ragged breath.

"I don't like it."

"What?"

"Your involvement in this."

"It's out of our control. It's the reason I'm here at all."

I stare into his eyes and smile. "Think about it. If it wasn't for Massimo and who I am, we would never have met. It's done both of us a favor really and we should celebrate that."

"Celebrate." He cocks his brow. "I like the sound of that."

"What do you have in mind?"

I can't prevent the delighted grin that's never far away when he's around and he presses me back onto the sheets and growls, "It involves fucking you all night long until you can't walk away from me."

"That's your plan?" I giggle.

"It's a good one, don't you think?"

"I think it's the best one I've ever heard."

He runs his hands under my top and lifts it off in one quick move and then makes short work of the skirt. As I lie quivering in my underwear, he rips off his own shirt and shrugs out of his pants and my breath hitches as I stare at the tribal beauty of my husband. He is living art. A book of delicious secrets and promises, cliff-hangers on every page enticing me to turn them eagerly to discover what happens next. I don't want this book to end; it must never end and as he pulls me up to meet his greedy lips, I feast on a dish I will never grow tired of.

There is an urgency in us that hasn't escaped me and as he kisses me as if it's our final ones, I have a need to show him how much he means to me.

This time, we make love. I know that because there is emotion wrapped around every touch, every lick and every thrust. He dances inside my body as if it's the paso doble. Hard, emotional and sexy. A master putting his servant in place and yet a coming together of equals. Loving, desire and worship are all present here and this dance of a lifetime is fast, hard and so beautiful it would stun any crowd watching. But this is us, two people in love, fighting to stay together because dancing with Ivan is a pleasure and a dream that I never want to wake up from.

He pulls me on top of him and as I grind against his cock, I watch his beautiful face and memorize every detail. I love this man wholeheartedly and nothing will tear us apart. I won't let it happen and as I perform my own lap dance of the most erotic kind, I feel so sexy, so free and so beautiful, as he gazes at me with adoration.

This time when he explodes inside me, it's without anything between us. As I drench his cock with my own release, we merge for the first time since we met. I know what this means, what could be the result of this, and I wonder if this was his plan all along. Join us together for eternity and make something so special we would do anything to protect it. Have we started our family tonight? I fucking hope so, because what we have is too good to let anything come between us.

Our sweat binds us together and his fingers tangle in my hair and as our beating hearts slow down, I whisper, "I love you, Ivan the savage."

"Ya lyublyu tebya, printsessa."

"What does that mean?"

"It means, I love you, princess."

This time when I kiss him, it's with the biggest smile on my face because now nothing can ever touch us and if my life doesn't include this man beneath me, then who wants to live, anyway?

CHAPTER 36

IVAN

When we wake in the morning, we have the place to ourselves.

The first thing I do when I open my eyes is lie and watch my wife while memorizing every detail of her face. I still can't believe I got so lucky. I don't deserve her. She is the most beautiful, innocent angel who shines like a star in a dark cave of depression.

Last night we discussed the plan and how we would achieve the impossible. To rid the world of Massimo Delauren and set us all free.

We got the call from Alessandro an hour after Charlotte left us. Massimo has been contacted, and the plan is set in place. Alessandro's grandfather has agreed to coordinate the exchange at a location in Sicily and Massimo is expected to arrive there in three days' time.

We are waiting to see if he bites, and my friends have all left to organize their troops.

Massimo will sustain an attack he must never survive and somehow, we must protect our women from getting caught up in the crossfire. That's why I'm so afraid for Charlotte, because if anything happened to her because of me, I may as well join her because I wouldn't want to live, anyway.

"Morning." Her voice sounds husky and edged in sleepy contentment and I capture her lips and kiss her deeply, loving the scent of my woman in my bed.

"Morning, malyshka, are you ready for me?"

"What now?" Her eyes snap open and without another word, I roll over and slide inside her sticky wet heat, loving the most satisfying kind of wake-up call.

Her gasp of pleasure fills my heart and I stroke her face while gazing into her beautiful blue eyes. With every thrust and every groan, I relish the sensation she creates and the flush of pleasure on her face makes me so happy I never want to leave.

We are so close nothing can come between us and as I make love to my wife, it's the best kind of start to my day.

Her orgasm hits her hard and I watch as her face explodes into one of such beauty I can only watch and admire as she rides the orgasm that I created.

My own isn't far away and as I shoot deep inside her, I hope one of them finds its mark. I want to watch her body swell with my child. I want a large family with the woman I love, and I hope she's up for that because the future I imagine with her is filled with laughter and fun. I will buy her that house on the water's edge and I will make her happy. It may be a little more guarded than most, but we will script our own future, which reminds me I still need to deal with my past first.

* * *

LEAVING CHARLOTTE TO TAKE A SHOWER, I head to the kitchen to fetch us a couple of coffees. Now everyone has left, there is a skeleton staff that always remains but I'm in no mood for conversation today.

I sense a storm approaching and can't shake the premonition that something is badly wrong. As I wait for the coffee machine to work its magic, I put in a call to my father, deciding to come clean and tell him I'm on my honeymoon and deal with the shit he throws when it lands.

Strangely, there's no answer and that worries me. There's always an answer, even if it's his hated voice on a message.

I must have the wrong number and try again, but for the second time, silence.

Feeling antsy, I call his second in command knowing that Konstantin will tell me where he is and once again, I'm met with silence.

I check my signal and note it's strong and briefly wonder if the lines are down in Russia. When I look again, I see a voice message I must have overlooked from my cousin, George. It's unusual for him to call me. We've never really been close, and he was the lucky one and got a desk job in the Kremlin rather than be sucked into the family business.

He simply asks me to call him as soon as I get the message, and something tells me this call will change everything.

This time he answers on the second ring and says urgently, *"Ivan."*

"What's happening? I can't reach my father." I don't hang around and he says in a low voice.

"Where are you?"

"Out of the country." The fuck I'm telling him where I am, and he sighs heavily.

"Thank God for that."

"Why?"

There's a short silence and then his voice softens, and he says with a deep sigh, *"I'm sorry, Ivan, your father was killed yesterday in a brutal attack."*

I hear his words, but they don't really register, and I don't know how to react. George fills in the silence and says in a grim voice, *"It was a consolidated attack on his home and businesses.*

They were all wiped out. There's nothing left." He falters before whispering, *"You no longer have a bratva family, Ivan. You're on your own."*

On my own. How I've longed to hear those words my entire life and George says urgently, *"Was it you? Was this your work? It's important to discover who did this."*

"You think I killed my own fucking family?"

I'm incensed because I've imagined slaughtering my father hundreds of times, but I would never harm the soldiers that have worked with us for many years. They are loyal and deserve protection, not to go down with the ship.

"I'm sorry I had to ask. It's just, well, there are questions being asked and the fact you were missing causes concern."

"I'm on my fucking honeymoon. Is that ok with the Kremlin?"

He laughs softly. *"Congratulations cousin, pass on my best wishes to your bride because she'll need all the help she can get."*

"So, what happens now?" My mind is racing at a million miles an hour and he says with a sigh.

"I'd stay where you are. The dust will settle and any inheritance you are owed will be paid into your account. You may want to organize a remembrance service when you return, but I would advise against a funeral until we find out who's responsible."

"Any ideas?" He must have one because he deals in secret shit for the Kremlin, and he sighs.

"Nobody is admitting to anything. It's a huge shock to everyone, which is why we thought of you. Leave it with me, I'll get to the bottom of it and in the meantime, enjoy your bride safe in the knowledge if you wanted to, you need never step foot in Russia again."

"Is that a warning?"

I know my cousin and there is always meaning behind his words, and he says abruptly, *"Wherever you are, Ivan, I hope it's somewhere well protected because things like this don't happen without warning. Something is going on, and Russia is not the safest place right now. Rival bratvas are edgy and looking over their shoulders. If you return, I'm guessing you won't make it out of the airport. Just stay safe cousin and I'll call you when it's clear to return home."*

He cuts the call, leaving me torn. On the one hand, I have suffered a huge loss—my family. Every single one of them are now dust. My home is gone, and I have no businesses. This is how it works. The government will step in and seize everything, and the only thing I will be left with is my father's personal wealth.

As I make the coffee on autopilot, my thoughts wrap around my soul like barbed wire and then a soft voice whispers in my ear as an angel catches me and slides her arms around my waist from behind.

"I missed you."

Knowing Charlotte is here makes everything immediately better and spinning around, I kiss her deeply and with a desperation that tells me I'm losing my grip.

She pulls away and looks up, gently trailing her fingers across my face, and whispers, "You look terrible. What happened?"

I'm not sure where to begin and, leaning back against the counter, I pull her close and say in a hoarse whisper, "It appears this is now our home."

"What do you mean?"

"My family are dead. Murdered in cold blood and our homes and businesses burned to the ground in a brutal attack."

Her eyes widen with horror, and she makes to speak and, shaking my head, I place my finger to her lips and say with a slight smile.

"Whoever's responsible did us a huge favor. I had no love for my father, and I have prayed for his death countless times. This has just saved me from doing the job myself."

She appears shocked and I shrug. "If that surprises you, it's because you never met him. I won't be mourning the bastard, but I will be mourning the soldiers who died with him."

"Where does that leave you — us?"

She looks worried and I laugh, causing her eyes to widen and I pull her in tightly against me and say, "It means we are free to buy your house, raise a family and live our dream. My father was a wealthy man and that will come to me. I may never need to work again and yet we both already know that will never happen. Now I will devote my life to making you happy and become an active participant in Club Mafia. I will assist my brothers any way I can with all the freedom of not having any ties back to Russia."

"You're really happy about this?"

She looks unconvinced and for the first time in my life, a huge weight falls from my shoulders and I grin.

"I'm more than happy, princess because now we get to travel, see the world and live our life by our own terms and conditions. The only thing standing in the way of that is your father and once this is over, we will both enjoy the same level of freedom without looking over our shoulders the entire time."

Charlotte beams with a happiness I won't completely share until her father joins mine and as we grab our coffees and head back to bed to enjoy them, I intend on making the most of every second we have together as if it's our last.

CHAPTER 37

WINTER

I'm so cold. My prison isn't its usual even temperature and I wonder if this is just another one of Massimo's mind games.

I have been locked in here for several days, which is unlike him. Usually, he likes to bring me out to play at least every other day, and I'm beginning to wonder if something's wrong. Is he even here? Did he go away somewhere? Is he dead?

Part of me hopes he is because it appears that's the only way of this mad marriage that I never asked for.

The only thing keeping me going is my son and picturing him upstairs in a nursery fit for a king is comforting because he is happy, content and well looked after and whoever's job that is, is doing a very good one.

I am never allowed to meet anyone unless Massimo allows it, but whenever I'm granted time with Frankie, he is always alone. Massimo permits me a few stolen nights when he is pleased with me and now I'm anxious because I haven't been given the chance to earn that precious time all the time I'm locked in here.

I have stopped counting the days, weeks, months, even. I'm

guessing we have been part of this world for close on two years now and every day is a life sentence. Sometimes I wonder about home. I try not to but at my lowest point, my brother creeps into my thoughts and gives me the power to survive. For Frankie, for Angelo and for Alessandro. The man who stole my heart along with my virginity and gave me the greatest gift of all — our son.

Not that he knows, of course. He must be carrying on with his life and I hope he is happy. Does he even remember me? I'm guessing he was angry when I married Massimo because, to the outside world, it's what I want. It's far from that and I am struggling to survive. There is only one thing keeping me sane, and that is saving my son.

Massimo is a monster. An evil bastard who will turn on Frankie one day. I have no doubt about that which is why I am constantly looking for my opportunity to save us both.

I never get one.

The only people in my daily life are the silent servants who bring me food and empty my waste bucket. There are no luxuries in Massimo's dungeons. The only time I live any kind of normal life is when he brings me out to play but now he has a much more interesting person to play with. For him, anyway.

On the odd occasion I'm allowed to stay in an actual room with all the luxuries he can afford. There is no communication with the outside world though—ever. Then he locks me in my dungeon when he has no time to spare me, or if I've displeased him in some way. I never know what's going on in his mind and just accept whatever he makes me do. I used to be strong, but that strength has been drained away carefully and over time, however I keep one hidden reserve deep inside for the opportune moment. The moment when I get my revenge.

He took delivery of his best friend six days ago. Wesley Vasquez. Flynn's father, as it happens. He betrayed him and Massimo is not big on forgiveness. At first, I endured the screams through the open doorway of the cell next to mine. I heard him pleading for his life while Massimo tortured him in revenge for something that happened over twenty years ago. He took Massimo's daughter from him and replaced her with Flynn. Just thinking of the pain my friend suffered because of that decision makes me relish the suffering of the man who caused it.

That was two days ago. Now the screams have become silent, and Massimo hasn't been back. Is Wesley dead? Is Massimo dead too? I wish I knew.

I must have fallen asleep because the sound of my cell opening brings me to my feet and my husband stands before me, appearing in a better mood than when he put me here.

"My darling, Winter, how I've missed you."

He approaches my cage and shakes his head. "We really need to get you cleaned up, my darling. Your hair is a mess and there is dirt on your face."

I feel an icy chill creeping over me because Massimo detests dirt. Any hint of imperfection sends him into a rage, and I wonder if this is just another one of his mind games to unsettle me.

He unlocks the cage and offers me his hand and as I take it, his hated fingers close around mine.

"Come, we will clean you up and then I have a special treat lined up for you."

My heart beats frantically in case it involves another dinner with one of my friends. I dread them like the plague because they rip my heart out every time. Knowing I can't react and must keep my fear and pain hidden because my role is to convince every single one of them I'm happy with my husband. If they suspect I'm not, they may try to rescue me and, knowing Massimo, I would be made to watch him cut them to pieces before my eyes. I play my part for their own safety, and it hurts like hell when I witness their shocked looks of pity, knowing there is nothing they can do to save me.

We wander to the dressing room and, as always, I stand on the pedestal in the center of the room while Massimo indulges his hobby of washing and dressing me like a human doll. He is never interested in me for sexual gratification. His preference is young men, but he does love to make up my face, style my hair and paint my nails. He selects the finest clothes from a room dripping with the best of everything, and it gives him great pride to parade me around on his arm in my role as his loyal, loving wife.

When we return, if I have pleased him, I earn a night with my son. If not, I am returned to my 'shelf' as he calls it and left there until required. This is my life, and I have learned to remove all emotion from my heart. There is no expectation and no hope for freedom. I just take each minute as it comes and hope I survive to the next one.

Once I am dressed in a pale blue trouser suit with matching nails and my hair swept up in an intricate updo, he says critically, "I had wanted to bleach your hair but as it turns out, there is no need for that."

I say nothing and walk with him through the corridors of his fortress and am surprised when he stops at the top of the staircase and says with excitement.

"I have something to show you. I think you'll like it."

I try to look interested, and he smiles, leaning forward and dropping the lightest kiss on my painted lips.

"So beautiful, my darling. An exquisite work of art. Now you will enjoy the rest of my art collection."

I follow him in surprise as he leads me to the other side of the staircase toward another one and as we reach the top, he presses his hand against the biometric entry system and the steel door slides open, revealing a huge room that is completely white. It resembles a hospital, but the chandeliers that hang from the ceiling tell of a much more luxurious place, and I gaze in awe at a magnificent gold chandelier designed like a statue, spinning around and shining as it catches the light.

It looks almost life sized, and I wonder how heavy it is. Is it pure gold? I wouldn't put that past my husband because he appears to have more money than sense and always enjoys the finest money can buy.

Beneath it is a glass chamber, and as we step across the room, Massimo grips my hand tightly and whispers, "I want you to meet someone special, Winter."

My heart almost gives out on me when I notice a body inside. It appears to be lying on white silk and there are fresh flowers placed carefully on top of it. I move closer and stare at the portrait of a beautiful woman hanging above it, surrounded by a solid gold frame and I hold my breath when I register how beautiful she was. Long blonde hair and brilliant blue eyes stare out of the painting with a soft smile on her ruby red lips. She is dressed in white. In fact, it looks like a wedding dress, and she is happy. I see it in her eyes.

"Meet Imogen, my wife."

Massimo sounds so proud, reverent even, and it's as if he's a different person entirely. He is humbled in front of this woman and as he stares up at her, I'm surprised when a small tear edges from his eye.

"I love her." His voice is soft, and I strain to listen as he whispers, "She is the most beautiful woman in the world. We are in love, aren't we, my darling?"

He stares at the painting and smiles and, for some reason, it breaks my heart.

"This is Winter. Remember I told you about her? She is my new toy."

He turns and says in a whisper, "Say hello to my wife, Winter, don't be shy."

"Um, hello Imogen. I'm, um, pleased to meet you."

The woman in the painting smiles down at me and then Massimo shocks me by lying flat against the glass and wailing as if he's in the greatest torment.

It feels so wrong to be here and I'm not sure what to do and then he stands up and says angrily, "My wife was murdered by our daughter. You heard the story. My beautiful wife gave her life so my daughter could live, and she was stolen from me before I could even meet her."

He stares at me, and I hate the madness in his eyes as he growls, "They think they are so clever. All of them. My former nanny, my best friend, and then your own friends from college."

The fear races through my blood like lava from a volcano as I sense change coming and he laughs like a maniac as he stutters, "But I am always one step ahead of them. You see, my darling Winter, they believe they have it all figured out. They want to set up an exchange. My daughter for you."

I almost take a step back because I wasn't expecting this. A lifeline, a chance to escape, and yet how would that possibly work?

"But Frankie." My voice comes out hopeful and yet resigned to having those hopes dashed and he says cruelly, "Stays with me."

"But ..." I'm uncertain what to do because one false move could end in torture for me, and I have been trained to listen and accept my fate. I must remember that and wait for him to reveal the whole picture, and then he startles me by pointing to the gold chandelier and laughs out loud.

"You remember Wesley, don't you, darling?"

I stare up in shock and witness the gold painted body of the man who betrayed Massimo so cruelly.

"I'm so happy with this new work of art that I created personally."

He moves beside me and holds my face roughly in his

hands, forcing me to gaze up at the twirling body of a man who suffered a bitter ending.

"I brought him as a gift for Imogen. She can look up and stare at the man who stole our baby." Suddenly, he laughs out loud. "Do you want to know the best thing about my newest creation, my darling?" I nod and he whispers, "He's still alive."

I glance up in horror as Massimo says with pride, "The line holding him up there is life support. It's keeping his body and mind active, but the gold paint has suffocated his skin. There is one bald patch on the top of his head where the line was drilled into and he spins on it, fully aware at all times, regretting the fact he betrayed me."

I think I'm going to pass out when he calls out, "Isn't that right, Wesley? You get to regret double crossing me for the rest of your miserable life. You remain alive all the time I say so and are a living work of art that I will treasure for the rest of my life."

Massimo cackles like the maniac he is. "You should have been there, Winter. To witness him pleading and begging for his life as I made him pay. It was interesting watching his body respond to the torture I inflicted on it. I even learned a few new skills that he can take the credit for. Yes, I have spent an enjoyable few days, my dear, creating this masterpiece for my wife's pleasure."

He forces me to look at the glass chamber and I almost gag when I see the mummified remains of the once beautiful creature who lives on in the painting.

"So, my darling, Winter, this is how I love. Nobody will ever get away from me, not anyone I adore, and you are no exception."

My heart dives straight to the floor as I struggle to cling on to any hope at all and he says with glee, "They think they are so smart using the Bratva to kidnap my daughter before I could save her. Spiriting her away and holding her for ransom in exchange for you."

He shakes his head and says in a childish voice, "Ring a ring of roses a pocket full of posies atishoo atishoo, they all fell down."

Then he laughs like the maniac he is and splutters, "They are all gone."

My heart freezes as I wait to hear something that will break me.

"I annihilated them all for daring to take my precious daughter from me. One by one, they fell and they don't even know it was me. Ingenious darling, don't you agree?"

I nod and smile as he always expects. "You are so clever, my darling."

The words stick in my throat, and he smiles with pleasure.

"I had an invitation today that I respectfully declined."

He looks at his wife's body and runs his hands across the glass chamber. "They offered for us to go to Sicily, to swap girls."

He throws his head back and laughs with amusement. "They thought I would be stupid enough to walk willingly into their trap. Honestly, I worry about them, they won't last long in this world. No, I know who has my daughter now and when they least expect it, I will liberate her. One by one they will hang in my dungeons, and I will have my pleasure. Five men all ripe for the picking who will be my new toys to play with. Don't worry, I'll allow you to watch while I rip them apart for both our pleasure. This is why they'll never win, because I am always several steps ahead of them. We'll remain here where we are safe and turn them against one another. Have no fear my darling Winter, my daughter will be returned to me but on my terms."

He looks around and says happily, "Then we will be a family again." He approaches his wife's body and smiles lovingly. "Did you hear that, Imogen darling? Our daughter will join you. I will place her chamber beside yours and she will keep you company, along with Wesley. We will all be together again and when Winter has served her purpose, I'm sure she will love hanging above our daughter and spinning for her pleasure. Yes, I can see it now, one big happy family."

He turns to me and says with a leer, "Don't worry about your son, my darling, Frankie and I will enjoy a different relationship. He will replace you as my most loved toy and I will have everything I ever wanted."

The horror of my situation is too much to bear, and I don't know how I hold it together to whisper the words he is expecting. "Thank you, my darling."

As he throws one last lingering look at the coffin and glances up at the spinning statue, he smiles with satisfaction.

"Yes, the future is looking good for all of us."

CHAPTER 38

CHARLOTTE

CLUB MAFIA

We watch the helicopters land, and I can already tell something isn't right.

"What's happening?"

I whisper to Ivan, who is stretched out beside me on the sun bed by the pool. For the last few days, we have treated our stay here as a honeymoon and I am more in love with my husband than ever. We spent our time making love and soaking up the sun, taking refreshing dips in the pool and generally acting like any other couple deeply in love. Our nights are spent wrapped in each other's bodies and exploring every possibility and every inch of one another.

The dreaded phone call never came and now we are being invaded, reminding me of the day this all started. No wonder I'm anxious, but Ivan just stretches out and says with a sigh, "It appears the boys are back in town."

"What boys?"

"Club Mafia."

He sighs and sitting up, peers at the sight with an irritable frown.

"We should get some clothes on. You can stay here if you like, but you may be more comfortable inside."

"You're probably right." Jumping up, I take his hand and we run back into the house and up to our bedroom.

As we shower and change, I can't stop the nerves from eating me up inside and Ivan must sense that because he pulls me close and when his strong arms wrap around me, I breathe a sigh of relief. As long as I'm in them, surrounded by his delicious form of close protection, nothing can hurt me.

We head downstairs to meet Ivan's friends and as we reach the living room, I notice that Angelo and Malik are deep in conversation by the fireplace. They look up as we enter, and I don't miss the serious expressions on their faces and wonder if I should leave them to talk.

Ivan grips my hand even tighter and says gruffly, "What's up?"

Angelo offers me a warm smile, but I don't miss the anxiety in his eyes as he says with a sigh, "The plan won't be going ahead. Massimo declined the invitation."

I stare at them in shock and yet it's as if he dealt me a knockout punch with a lifeline attached.

"He doesn't want to see me?"

My eyes are wide because I wasn't expecting this and for a moment Angelo looks sorry for me. Not that he should, because I don't even know this man and the fact he doesn't want to meet me fills me more with relief than disappointment.

Ivan growls, "The bastard. He guessed it was a trap."

"I would have been more surprised if he agreed."

Malik sighs. "It was always a possibility, and he is playing a cunning game. His answer came with an open invitation for

Charlotte to visit him whenever she is ready. She only has to call, and he will arrange transportation."

He looks at me pityingly. "He forwarded his personal number to be passed onto you but said his wife would not be able to survive without him and had requested to stay."

Angelo hisses, "I'm not sure what game he is playing, but there is no way in hell Winter would elect to stay with that bastard. There is something more to this, which is why we're here."

We all look up when the door opens, and Flynn arrives, but he's not alone.

When I see the man beside him, my heart twists and then plummets to the depths of my soul. This man is darkness personified. Like Ivan, he is heavier than the rest, a solid mass of muscle that clothing can barely contain, and his black hair is pulled in a tight ponytail behind his head. His dark turbulent eyes flash in my direction and my mouth dries and I lose the power of speech in an instant.

Ivan confirms what I'm thinking when he says with a hint of emotion, "Alessandro."

He breaks away and I watch with tears in my eyes when he hugs his friend, and I can tell the feeling is mutual. Of all his friends, Ivan considers Alessandro his closest one and I'm guessing he is emotional because of what he's going through. Ivan told me he had a connection with Winter and has given up his future as a Hollywood director to re-join his grandfather's organization in Sicily.

Once again, the word mafia whispers like a demon of hell around my soul, coaxing me in and promising dark times ahead. Of all of them, Alessandro plays this part well because this man fucking terrifies me.

He steps back and as his eyes find mine, my breath hitches at the emotion in them and he looks at Ivan and shakes his head, before crossing the room to stand before me. If I thought he would be angry, I was wrong because he holds out his hand and says in a deep voice, "You must be Charlotte. Welcome to the family."

As I take his hand, I relish the power of his grip and remember Ivan telling me fondly of the fights the two of them enjoyed, making me wonder if I've married a madman. "I'm sorry..." My voice sounds small and hesitant, and he shakes his head. "There is nothing to be sorry about. Maybe your marriage, but I'm sure you'll figure out a way to rid yourself of that burden one day."

Ivan growls, "Are you spoiling for a fight, Beast?"

To my surprise, Alessandro just winks at me before turning to his friends and greeting them one by one.

As I sense the love in this room, I try to swallow the lump forming in my throat as, for just a moment, they shut me out. They are so happy to be together, it's obvious and once again my heart breaks for the reason they are here. One of their own is missing. A very important part of their tight knit family and now I understand why they are so desperate to bring her back. It must be wounding their souls at the thought of her living in hell and there is little they can do to help her. My own resolve hardens, and I vow to play my part because if I do nothing else in life, I want to change the look in their eyes and see them reunited with a woman who means the world to them all and so I say sharply, "How can I help?"

For the first time I don't buckle under the attention of the five dark lords that bring fear into a room and Ivan looks so proud it makes me happy.

Angelo's expression softens, and he says with a sigh, "We could all use a drink and grab a seat. We need to work out where we go from here."

As he organizes that, we take our seats in couches set around the huge fireplace and I snuggle against my husband, thankful his strength will help me through this.

He whispers, "You don't have to do anything, princess, this isn't your fight."

"If it's your fight, it's mine, and that will never change."

The hunger in his eyes matches my own and for a moment we shut the others out and then I feel bad when I see the pain in Alessandro's eyes as he watches us, and I guess it must be due to his own situation which makes my heart physically ache.

I take Ivan's hand and rest it in my lap and stare around the room, waiting to offer any help I can.

Once everyone has their drinks, Angelo says with a sigh. "We need a new plan. It's obvious Massimo has rightly guessed it was a trap and even the fact we offered him his daughter it wasn't enough to flush him out. Which makes me wonder what he's planning."

Malik nods. "I'm guessing he's taking a different approach, and the attack on the Bratva got me thinking."

All eyes turn to Ivan, whose eyes flash with anger, and he growls, "I will fucking end his life personally in revenge for the loss of my soldiers, though I may thank him first for ridding me of my father before I send him to join him in hell."

I'm not shocked by this statement, and neither are the others, it seems, probably because they all suffered abusive childhoods in much the same way and it kind of makes me understand them a lot more.

What must it be like to live this life from birth, knowing you have no control over what your father does to you? I can't imagine the horrors they've lived with all these years, and I offer a silent prayer of thanks to the people responsible for sending me to England. I escaped this torment and yet as I glance across the room at Flynn and he offers me a reassuring smile, I feel personally responsible for his own part in this madness.

All eyes turn to Alessandro when he says darkly, "We are

ready to take the fight to Massimo. I have the backing of my family and we are on standby to do whatever is necessary."

Angelo nods and I see a different expression in his eyes when he stares around at his friends and says gravely, "Alessandro's right. We need to take the fight to him. It's obvious Massimo isn't going to play by our rules and word has reached us he is the man responsible for wiping out Ivan's family. We will all be next; I am in no doubt about that because he knows we are coming for him. So, this is the plan."

As we listen to Angelo outlining something that could backfire on us spectacularly it makes me anxious. I understand this is something that needs to happen, but if it goes wrong, it could finish Club Mafia for ever.

* * *

MUCH LATER, when the details have been discussed and considered from every angle, we head off to bed and as the door closes on the world, Ivan holds me in his arms.

"Are you ok, malyshka?"

"Not really, I'm worried."

He kisses me softly and whispers, "We will be fine. Remember, we enjoy the best protection there is."

"Which is?"

"Love and loyalty. Massimo has loyalty born out of fear and they are very different when faced with a life changing decision. I know this is risky, but we have a strong army and the advantage is on our side and we will plan for every eventuality. Malik will second guess Massimo's moves and after what Alessandro told us, we have the identity of the one person who can flush Massimo out of his gilded cage."

Thinking back on the excitement in the room when Alessandro told us what he discovered, I wonder about the woman they must approach for help.

"Will she agree?"

Ivan nods and a triumphant smile breaks out across his face.

"Of course she will."

As he kisses me so deeply, it banishes every thought from my head other than what's coming next, and as we take this moment to bed, I am a lot more hopeful than before. Whatever happens next will change nothing between us. When this is over, we will start again. I will return home and introduce Ivan to my parents and then we will make a life together and enjoy creating a family because Club Mafia is now as much part of me as it is them, and if we need to fight for that, then bring it on.

EPILOGUE

ALESSANDRO

TWO DAYS EARLIER – SICILY

The past two years have been bittersweet. They have been the worst of my life and the best.

Now it's all set to change because the best part of my life will be sacrificed to change the worst. The one thing I want more than anything. To save Winter and bring her back to us.

I would say, back to me, but we never really got started. One night only was all we had, but it was a night that changed my life.

They say love can't happen like a bolt of lightning. Lust maybe, but never love.

I disagree.

I love Winter with all my heart because I have never got over losing her and I can't bear to look at women with similar features. I only employ blondes because they are nothing like my dark, exotic beauty.

I crave any mention of her, and I can't sleep at night

worrying about whose arms she lies in. It's the ultimate torture but I am getting used to it. It's woven into the fabric of my life, making me wear the pain. The only antidote to that was I got to live my dream.

I was set free from a life of madness to step into a different one. Strings were pulled on my behalf, and I found myself directing a movie that won an Oscar fresh out of the trap. I was up and coming and one to watch, and the past two years have been hard in a number of ways. I rarely sleep and I work too hard to drive all the images away in my head of the girl I loved and lost so cruelly.

We have tried so hard to bring her back to us. The plan was shaping up nicely and our positions of power are almost complete. Then Flynn learned our enemy has a daughter, and it changed everything. We thought we had won. We had the golden goose and then Massimo changed the game overnight.

"Buonasera, signor Majerio."

"Buonasera Tommaso."

I move past the respectful soldier who stands aside to let me pass and let the familiar settle around me like a well-worn cloak.

My grandfather's home. The head office of his Sicilian empire that my own father didn't think he could take on. He fled to Boston and started his own branch of our family, but my grandfather always had me marked as his heir apparent. I was told I reminded him of himself, and he wanted me to leave Rockwell and begin my training. I resisted, and it takes a very foolish person to go against my grandfather, but as it happened, he was feeling generous that day. I was given a respite on the understanding I would take over as the head of this family when he died or was unable to command. I enjoyed two years of freedom, but that has all changed now.

I'm here to take my place by his side for only one reason. Bringing Winter home.

The plan was to use my grandfather's connections to back us up and give us a formidable army behind us. It was meant to take place here in Sicily, but Massimo has changed all that and blocked our move.

Now I must convince my grandfather that I know what I'm doing if we are to stand any chance of pulling this off and so as I head into the den where he enjoys a pre-dinner cigar, I set my attitude to bastard.

"Alessandro."

His voice reaches me through the haze of smoke, and I smile when I hear the husky tones of a man who always appears as if he knows everything. I think he does, and my heart quickens when he points to the leather wing-backed chair opposite him and offers me a cigar.

"Brandy and cigars. My guilty pleasure above many others."

His gruff laughter makes me smile and, as I light the tip and take a drag of the pungent smoke, I settle into my role.

Handing me a glass of brandy, he raises his glass to mine. "So, we celebrate."

"We have something to celebrate?"

He laughs softly. "You tell me."

"We will celebrate when Massimo Delauren is dead, Nonno."

"Ah, your greatest enemy."

He puffs on his cigar, appearing in a thoughtful mood, and I wait for him to speak.

"Ma-ss-im-o." He drags out every syllable of his name and I swear every one of them grates on my nerves.

"He has been tolerated for far too long."

"So, you'll help us."

"You know my price."

"It's why I'm here." I regard him coolly and he nods, apparently satisfied.

"Your first plan has changed, I understand."

"He declined your invitation."

My grandfather sighs heavily.

"An unfortunate response because now we must play plan B, as they say."

"Which is?"

I'm guessing he has one because he hinted at that and he nods, slowly blowing out the smoke as if he hasn't a care in the world.

I envy him that.

"A good friend of mine has offered to assist with our problem."

"Do I know him?" I'm intrigued, as my grandfather laughs softly. "Her, Alessandro. Portia Symmons is her name. She runs a modeling agency in Los Angeles close to Massimo's home, well one of them, anyway."

I lean forward as he takes a swig of his drink and sighs happily.

"She was the woman who introduced Massimo to Imogen, his first wife. She modeled for Portia and was the most beautiful woman in many years. She was in great demand, but Massimo fell hard and soon they were married, and she worked no more."

He shakes his head. "The life of a mafia wife is not a free one, and she spent her days closely protected from his many enemies. Sadly, it was Mother Nature who claimed her life, and that is a force Massimo has no control over, no matter how hard he tries."

"So how can she help us?" I'm mystified and my grandfather arches his brow and looks disappointed. "Open your eyes, Alessandro, and look for the opportunity. It helps to understand everything possible about your enemy and I have investigated yours so hard I even discovered how much he weighed when he was born."

I feel foolish because my grandfather is a master at this, and I must remember that and will have everything worked out down to the finest detail.

"They meet once a month at Scarpetta in Beverly Hills. Massimo has a great love of fashion and adores his monthly conversations with somebody who shares his hobby. Portia is the best at what she does and has several high-profile celebrities among her many clients. Massimo loves to wallow in the shine that glamor provides, and Portia indulges him because he is her biggest benefactor."

He leans forward and I see the evil glint in his eyes as he says softly, "Portia has become increasingly worried about Massimo's state of mind. She senses he's sliding into madness at a breakneck speed. She is no longer comfortable around him and has offered to help us remove him from life."

"Why would she do that? She could be working for him and can't be trusted."

My grandfather just laughs before taking another lungful of cigar smoke.

"Did I mention she is my mistress?"

For a moment I just stare at him in awe because for fuck's sake, my grandfather must be approaching seventy years old.

He merely winks and clips the cigar and places it back in the box and lifting his glass, he drains it in one huge gulp. I watch the excitement blaze from his eyes as he says with a chuckle, "Just don't tell Nonna, otherwise she'll insist on accompanying me on my next trip there."

I'm not sure how I feel about this because I always thought my grandfather adored his wife and they were happily married.

He must sense my disapproval because he shrugs. "It's nothing. Just something to make a business trip more pleasurable. Portia knows the score and believe it or not, so does Nonna."

"She knows!"

"Not the details, but she resigned herself to my wandering eye years ago. When you are in my position, you are faced with a great deal of temptation. It's so easy to have what you want, and it takes a strong man to resist that. Portia is a fine-looking woman who knows how to please a man. Nonna can't be bothered anymore."

Now I feel nauseous and leaning back in my chair, say with a sigh. "Finish your story."

He laughs at my obvious discomfort and says quickly, "Portia will ask Massimo to bring his wife to the next meeting. She will say she's curious to meet her. We will book every seat in the restaurant and fill them with our men, and one very special diner will arrive with her new husband."

"Charlotte?"

He nods. "We will position her in his view and, using her as a distraction, we will cut the head off the snake."

"It sounds too easy." I think he may have underestimated Massimo and he shrugs. "Sometimes it's better not to overcomplicate things. Massimo won't be expecting an ambush because it's a regular arrangement. While he's dining with his wife and his close friend, you must instruct your friends to use their soldiers and strike his homes, businesses and wipe every trace of Massimo from life."

"This is huge." I'm astonished by the magnitude of my grandfather's plan, and he nods, his lips twisting into the evil grin that earned him his reputation.

"We must go in heavy and leave nothing to chance. Massimo will not leave that restaurant alive. You have my word on that."

He stands and nods toward the door. "It's time to eat and Nonna will be angry if we are late. Come, let us enjoy a family meal and talk about more agreeable things and welcome you home where you belong."

As he slings his arm around my shoulder, it's as if I just

struck a deal with the devil. I have traded my soul and I would do it again in a heartbeat if it brings Winter back to me.

* * *

THE NEXT DAY I leave for Club Mafia to inform my friends of the change of plan and to set the wheels in motion of devastation that will bring Massimo Delauren and his empire to a bitter end. But most of all, it will set Winter free and there is a tiny shred of hope in my heart that she will feel the same and our one night only will turn into the start of something beautiful – for both of us.

* * *

Thank you for reading Club Mafia–The Savage
The next book in the series is
Club Mafia – The Beast

If you want to know what happened at Rockwell Academy read Club Mafia–The Contract.

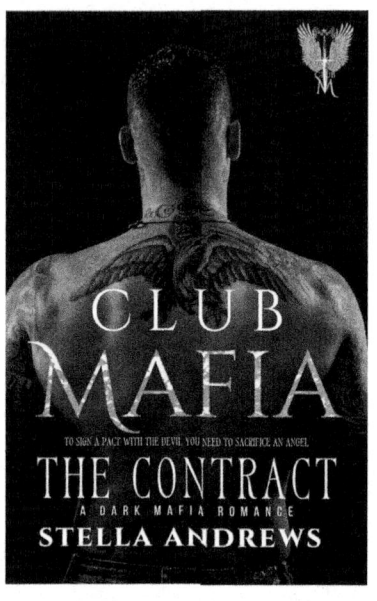

If you haven't read Angelo's story
Club Mafia~The Boss

Thank you for reading this story.
If you have enjoyed the fantasy world of this novel, please would you be so kind as to leave a review on Amazon?

Join my closed Facebook Group

Stella's Sexy Readers

Follow me on Instagram

Carry on reading for more Reaper Romances, Mafia Romance & more.
Remember to grab your free book by visiting stellaandrews.com.

ALSO BY STELLA ANDREWS

Twisted Reapers

Sealed With a Broken Kiss
Dirty Hero (Snake & Bonnie)
Daddy's Girls (Ryder & Ashton)
Twisted (Sam & Kitty)
The Billion Dollar baby (Tyler & Sydney)
Bodyguard (Jet & Lucy)
Flash (Flash & Jennifer)
Country Girl (Tyson & Sunny)

The Romanos
The Throne of Pain (Lucian & Riley)
The Throne of Hate (Dante & Isabella)
The Throne of Fear (Romeo & Ivy)
Lorenzo's story is in Broken Beauty

Beauty Series
*Breaking Beauty (Sebastian & Angel) ***
Owning Beauty (Tobias & Anastasia)

ALSO BY STELLA ANDREWS

Broken Beauty (Maverick & Sophia) *
Completing Beauty – The series

Five Kings
Catch a King (Sawyer & Millie) *
<u>Slade</u>
Steal a King
Break a King
Destroy a King
Marry a King
Baron

Club Mafia
Club Mafia – The Contract
Club Mafia – The Boss
Club Mafia – The Angel
Club Mafia – The Savage
Club Mafia - The Beast

Standalone
The Highest Bidder (Logan & Samantha)
Rocked (Jax & Emily)
Brutally British
Deck the Boss

Reasons to sign up to my mailing list.

• A reminder that you can read my books FREE with Kindle Unlimited.
• Receive a monthly newsletter so you don't miss out on any special offers or new releases.
• Links to follow me on Amazon or social media to be kept up to date with new releases.
• Free books and bonus content.

ALSO BY STELLA ANDREWS

•Opportunities to read my books before they are even released by joining my team.
•Sneak peeks at new material before anyone else.

stellaandrews.com
Follow me on Amazon

Printed in Great Britain
by Amazon